Romance
in
Evergreen

Romance in Evergreen

(Heart of Evergreen Book 2)

By

Mary L. Schmidt

Romance In Evergreen
Mary L. Schmidt
Copyright © 2024

by Mary Schmidt (M. Schmidt Productions)

All rights reserved.

Book and cover painting and design by Mary L. Schmidt

BISAC Subject Headings:
Fiction / Christian / Romance / Suspense
Fiction / Crime
Fiction / Thrillers / Psychological

Library of Congress
ISBN- Paperback 979-8-9903262-0-0
ISBN-13: eBook 979-8-9903262-1-7

CHRYSLER, DODGE, JEEP®, RAM, MOPAR®, SRT copyright FCA US LLC (FCA)

Land Rover® Tata Motors (India)

Bentley® Volkswagen

Nothing in this book was written with artificial intelligence. The characters are the from the author's own, real-life memoir, Her Heart, and others Christmas in Evergreen, both written by Mary L. Schmidt, and the rest in the author's imagination. Scenes used are either real-life or make-believe. Certain medical issues are from the author's own real-life experiences; thus, I wrote them as my reality.

First edition published May 31, 2024

Blog (https://www.whenangelsfly.net)
Facebook (https://www.facebook.com/MMSchmidtAuthorGDDonley)
Twitter (https://twitter.com/MaryLSchmidt)
Deviant Art (http://mschmidtartwork.deviantart.com/)

Table of Contents

Dedication

Always to Shane, and Sammy, who taught us so much about life, bravery, and that a baby and a five-year-old can be wiser beyond their brief time on Earth,

Always to Gene, our son, who we cherish so much, and has been wise beyond his years, and has turned into a kind man,

Always to Michael, my beloved husband, partner, and best friend in the entire world,

Always to Mary, my beloved wife, partner, and best friend in the entire world.

Prologue

"What did you just say? The senior officer (Special Agent Thompson) of the two men from Homeland Security, that both Nancy and Kim knew prior, repeated, 'Rob and Liza Caldwell were taken out as a hit' in Boston last night and we think their assassin is the agent handler extraordinaire, who put out the hit job on the President, and on you, Kim, last November. The hit man's name is Jeffrey Sanders, we do not know any alias, ethnicity, or if male or female. Security cameras were disabled before the actual hit. Rob and Liza were asleep when it happened early this morning. A silencer was used, and neighbors heard their dog barking non-stop and became worried. The couple checked on them, found them dead in their bed, and called 911. The police detectives could tell it was a professional hit and called us. Special Agent Hughes and I flew directly here from Washington, DC. A note left at the scene read, 'Two down, eleven to go' and the eleven to go are both of you, the President, and people unidentified. Make no mistake. The hit man will take out anyone with you, when, NOT if, they find you."

"How dare you take out my two best assets! I am coming for you, Kim, and your friend, Nancy! Never mind, my best assets died in a roll-over accident! They were after you, Kim! Now I am going to finish the job! Both of you and yours are going down! I know where you are and who you have in your life! Tit for tat. The same back to both of you!"

PART 1

Chapter One

"What did you just say? The senior agent (Special Agent Thompson) of the two men from Homeland Security, that both Nancy and Kim knew from their prior lives in Boston, repeated, 'Rob and Liza Caldwell were taken out as a hit in Boston last night and we think their assassin is the agent handler extraordinaire, who put out the hit job on the President, and the hit on Kim.' Special Agent Hughes and I flew directly here from Washington, DC, immediately."

*N*ancy's full pink lips and mouth gaped open, then closed, and opened again. "Kim, come down to the showroom, now!" She yelled out, her face ashen, and blue eyes wide open.

'The Gallery Loft of Evergreen' was Kim's heart in the world of art and creativity. Kim stepped lightly down the stairs from her art gallery's second floor, all five feet, three inches of her trim body sporting seafoam green eyes, and curly blonde hair that bounced with each step.

"What is up, Nancy? Need some help?" With a paint brush in hand, a smock over her top, and sporting dark blue skinny jeans with rugged black leather boots, Kim stopped dead in her tracks when she saw the two men. Fear gripped her heart and lungs tightly, and she barely breathed as she stared at both men.

Oh my…no…never…not again…why are those men here of all places…fear caused her blood to feel like ice as it coursed through her jarred and shocked body… Steve and Gary are dead, killed in the accident…Nancy and I are safe now…no assassins are after us, no assassin is after ME…both died in that wreck…both bodies had positive identification…this is not happening…it can't be happening…NO…

"

Steve and Gary are dead…get a grip now, Kim…close your eyes…then reopen… only Nancy will be there…except they were there…

Agent Thompson repeated, *"I'm so sorry to bring you this news, but Rob and Liza Caldwell were taken out as a hit in Boston last night, we think their assassin is the* agent handler extraordinaire, who put out the hit job on the President, and also the hit on you, Kim, last November."

Nancy's hands and chin quivered and ran both hands through her short dark pixie cut hair. "Why do you think it was a hit man who killed our friends? Steve and Gary are dead, and that story, that chapter of our lives, is over. We left Boston behind when we moved to Evergreen, Colorado." Visibly shivering in shock, Nancy grabbed her slip-over jacket and wrapped herself inside it, wishing this were a simple dream, and knowing trouble loomed ahead.

It was the end of May and Memorial Day weekend, yet Nancy was chilled to the bone. *I'm dizzy…not again…never again…I simply can't do this…why did I ever marry my dead ex – Gary Moore…not again, Lord, please make this go away…I only want my man, Richard, and children someday soon… please not this yet again…I want a baby so bad…but not with this happening…*

"Rob and Liza were killed full-on hit style." Agent Thompson replied with concern in his voice as Agent Hughes peered out the front windows of the art gallery.

Shocked, Kim asked, "Do you think that hit man knows where we are? Is that why you are here? Agent Hughes keeps looking out the front gallery windows! You turned the closed sign facing out, and the doors are locked as far as I can tell. I am more perceptive and cognizant of my surroundings now." Kim glared into Agent Thompson's eyes and her eyes dared him to speak the truth. She had had it with this cloak-and-dagger-spy-game and had moved on in life. *Or so she thought…*

"Has the nightmare come back to us in our new location? Tell me NOW!!!" Kim demanded as she reeled in shock and felt zero comfort. *It was all her fault that Rob and Liza were now dead…had she never gone to them for help, they would be alive…she had caused Rob and Liza's deaths…this was on her, and her alone…she was guilty of their deaths…Nancy was innocent…she didn't run for her life like I did…I ran to Rob for help…and now they are both dead… survivors guilt…maybe…but this is my fault…*

"No!" Nancy's blue eyes were wide open just as much as her mouth was. "This is not a funny joke! Not at all!" *These men are NOT here, and she was in a horrible nightmare of a dream…she only needed to wake up…yet they were here, and it was a living nightmare…in real time…like now…*

"It's not a joke," he replied. "I am so sorry. The assassin left a cryptic note that read 'Two down, twelve to go!' and we think the note might refer to both of you, the President, and others. The President is safe and has extra secret service agents around him. No one can reach him. We flew straight here in a military jet."

Kim sat down abruptly at the coffee and tea counter by the cash register and shook her head. Her green eyes stared intently at the agent, and she demanded in a remote but cold tone, "What are you not telling us? I want details, and I want the details now!"

Rob and Liza never deserved to be killed in this cruel manner. If only she hadn't asked Rob for help…it was her fault…and now they were dead…her worst nightmare had reared its ugly head once again…and it was all her fault, entirely…she was to blame…If she hadn't married Steve, none of this would have happened…it's all my fault…maybe survivors guilt…even so, it's entirely my fault…

"The name we have is Jeffrey Sanders, has many aliases, no priors, of unknown ethnicity, or if male or female. Security cameras were disabled before the actual hit. Rob and Liza were asleep when it happened early this morning. A silencer was used, and neighbors heard their dog barking non-stop and became worried. The couple checked on them, found them dead in their bed, and called 911." Agent Thompson explained as gently as he could.

"The police detectives could tell it was a professional hit and called Homeland Security. We read the report, and knew we had to fly out to both of you immediately. If it helps to give any comfort at all, Rob and Liza never knew what hit them, they died instantly with no pain, and they were asleep when they died. We flew directly here. The twelve to go are both of you and other unknowns for now. Make no mistake! The hit man will take out anyone with you, when, *NOT* if, they find you." Agent Thompson gazed at both women, and he felt bad that he was the one to bring them the horrific news. *They had to be told, though.*

"This is not happening! No way!" Nancy yelled. "You cannot simply walk in here and tell us about Rob and Liza, just like that! No!"

Pure evil reared its ugly head…a wave of dizziness washed over her, and she reached for the counter…dear Lord, why now…no…I can't do this again…please give me the strength to carry on and get the facts from these agents…and to deal with what they say…all I want is a baby and my life would be complete…

"So, you are telling us that a professional hit person is after us, and will kill anyone with us at any given time and place? Really?" Kim felt for her black Ruger under the counter and found little comfort in touching it.

It was loaded, though, the safety was on, and she knew how to use it thanks to that hit man of a husband who tried to kill her…back in Boston…her previous life she'd run from…the one who might have caused the death of her parents… and now…after being married to the love of her life, Paul, for only five months… fear gripped her entire being…Dr. Paul and Kim Smith…was this the end of their beautiful love story or not…

The agent solemnly agreed in the affirmative. "We are here to provide backup for both of you. To do so, we need to ask questions so that we can figure out a plan to help you and those close to you. Our goal is to keep all of you safe and alive. This means the gallery is closed until safety has been established and the hit man caught or killed."

Nancy's tall and slender frame shuddered as she thought about their loved ones being at risk. *Talk about curveballs…this one hit it out of the park and right back in as a sucker punch to her gut…she wanted to double over but knew she must keep her wits strong…keep your faith, girl…faith…*

Chapter Two

"What would you do if you found out you were the next target on a professional hit man's list?"

Chills washed over and through her body as Nancy realized that she must call her boyfriend that she had been dating since last New Year's Eve, and a highly skilled wood carver, Richard Manse. "Kim, you must call your husband, Dr. Paul, and the Leawood's. I am calling Richard now."

Both Homeland Security agents nodded in agreement. The senior agent told them that they were safe in the gallery for now, and that those who were called should come to the gallery ASAP. Extra agents were outside the gallery and in the general area, some of them snipers, and the area was secured.

Richard, a rugged dark haired, and bearded mountain man answered on the first ring. Cheerfully he answered the call, "Good morning, my lovely Nancy. The gallery must be busy since it is a Saturday."

"Oh, Richard. You must drop what you are doing and come here right now. You must do this ASAP. Special agents from Homeland Security are here." Nancy wanted to cry, but she stood rooted in her spot and trembled. Agent Thompson gently took the phone from Nancy's clutch.

"Wait, what? Are you serious?" Richard asked as Agent Thompson got on the phone.

"This is Agent Thompson. We have a situation, and you must come to 'The Gallery Loft of Evergreen' immediately. Do not ask questions now. Stay calm, we are in control, and no one is in danger as the area has been secured."

"On my way now. Be there in ten minutes." Richard was confused. What are government agents doing at Kim's art gallery? What kind of danger? This must have something to do with Nancy's prior life in Boston and her ex – Gary Moore. But how? Gary Moore was dead, and dead people never come back to life – except in the movies!

Kim reached out to her husband of just over five months, Dr. Paul Smith, a neurosurgeon, and he answered on the first ring. "Hi, Kim! The trout are not biting in Bear Creek, so I think I will call it a day. Can I treat you to lunch in Evergreen?" he queried his wife, hoping she would take him up on his offer.

"No, Paul. I am so, so, so sorry. It is all my fault that you are now involved in this mess. I never should have married you. What was I thinking? It is my fault! I never should have moved to Evergreen! It is all my fault! It is all on me!" Kim cried out and Agent Thompson took her cell phone and put it to his own ear.

"What are you talking about, Kim?" Paul was confused and he did not understand what she meant by the word "involved" or how, why, and what was her fault.

"This is Agent Thompson from Homeland Security. I need you to come to the art gallery immediately. Drive normally and come straight here, no stops on the way. Be careful and be aware of all things around you."

"What?" Paul asked, bewildered, and flummoxed.

"No questions until you are at the gallery. Please follow directions and come to the gallery now." Agent Thompson instructed Paul. "Stay safe, goodbye, and see you soon."

Paul's phone showed that Kim's had hung up. Last year, only six months ago, Kim had told him what had happened in Boston, and worried, he jumped in his Land Rover and headed back up the canyon towards Evergreen.

Paul never saw the large black dual cab truck, with a black bull bar in the front, hit him at an angle that directly threw his Land Rover over and into a rocky and briar-filled ravine coming to rest on the passenger side, driver's side wheels spinning in the air.

Two hikers saw the accident happen and the huge black truck drove away as fast as it could. They never got a license plate number as they ran to the ravine and made their way down.

One hiker, Greg, was an EMT (Emergency Medical Technician), and he felt Paul's wrist for a pulse. It was weak and the lone victim was not breathing.

"David, I need your help. We must extricate this man immediately!" Greg yelled to his friend.

"Coming! I called 911," David replied as he climbed up to the now-top-of-the-truck, the driver's side. The Land Rover moved a bit as he scrambled to the top.

"We must stay safe as we work so put most of your weight on the north part of the SUV. Together we will extricate this man. David, I need you to help me hold his neck and head straight as we pull him out through the driver's window and lay him flat on the driver's side (top) of the truck. Ready?"

"Understood. I am ready, Greg. Let us do this," David reached down to secure and brace the victim's head and neck as best he could.

Together, they got the victim out and on his back against the driver's side. Thankfully, spontaneous breathing started, and Paul regained consciousness. The air bag had knocked the wind out of him when it went off.

'What ha…," Paul tried to speak as dizziness washed over him.

"You were in an accident. My name is Greg, and I am an EMT. Can you tell me your name, sir?"

"Paul Smith", and then he lost consciousness again.

"David, I need you to keep his head and neck straight. He has a head injury." As Greg spoke, he thought of the man he was assessing, he knew the victim as Dr. Paul Smith, an ER doctor at the hospital he regularly took ambulance patients to.

Greg carefully and quickly checked Paul's pulse (now fast), looked at the pupils of both eyes (reactive), and raised his shirt to note how both sides of his chest moved as he could have a punctured lung (even-no puncture).

"Keep him still, David. I must stabilize his right leg now." Greg moved lower and positioned the right leg next to the left leg so that the obvious compound fracture in his right leg was as stable as could be.

Then Greg tied his hoodie as a bandage on the open part of the broken leg to stem the flow of blood, and to decrease further contaminants getting into the open wound with bones visible.

"That hurts bad!" Paul said, when his leg was moved. "I hit my head on something in the vehicle."

"You will be okay, Dr. Smith. Do you recognize me?" Greg asked. It was imperative to know how lucid Paul truly was.

"I know you, Greg. Thanks for helping me. I do not know how I ended up in this ravine. Tell me your assessment, head to toe."

"You have a compound fracture of your right leg; I have stabilized it the best way possible currently. I have a hoodie tied around your open right leg wound so further debris does not get inside, and to help stem the bleeding. Your lungs are good, no signs of a lung puncture. The air bag knocked the wind out of you but after extrication, spontaneous breathing began. Pulse is fast, but steady. Pupils are reactive. My friend, David, is keeping your neck and head braced."

"Has 911 been called?" Paul asked and the answer to that question could be heard as the sirens grew louder.

"They are here, doctor. Can you tell me what day it is, where you were going, and if you have any bleeding disorders?" Greg replied, as he kept reassessing Paul."

"It is Saturday of Memorial Day weekend, and I was headed to Evergreen. I have no bleeding disorders." Paul responded as the ambulance arrived.

Two EMT's braced and stabilized the Land Rover so it would safely stay in position while Greg gave the pertinent information to them. Once the vehicle was stable, one EMT climbed up with a neck and head brace in hand.

"I'll move out of your way," David told the EMT.

"No," the EMT replied. "You stay where you are and keep doing what you are doing, until I have this head and neck brace secured in place, and I'll tell you when you can safely move away." The EMT worked carefully and got Paul's head and neck braced securely. David was finally able to move out of the way and off the Land Rover.

Stunned, David now realized he had just found out the steps to take, and not do, if he came upon a wreck in the future and no EMT Greg was with him. Could he do what Greg did? No. Did he know how to safely extricate and keep one's head and neck stable? Yes. Valuable lesson learned. Could he stay calm throughout? Yes. *Maybe…*

The EMT's worked efficiently and secured Paul on a rescue board, strapped him down, and carried him to the waiting ambulance.

Once inside, Paul asked for a phone. He wanted to call Kim and let her know he was safe and what had happened. She would worry that he had not arrived in Evergreen, yet.

Greg phoned Kim at the gallery, and she answered. "Hi, Kim. My name is Greg, and I am with your husband, Dr. Paul Smith, now. He has been in a motor vehicle accident, but he is okay. His leg is broken, and the ambulance is ready to leave for Lakewood. He is going to be fine so please do not worry." Greg heard the phone drop and then a man came on the line.

"This is Agent Thompson from Homeland Security. Are you Dr. Paul Smith?" Agent Thompson asked as he looked at Kim and saw the shock on her face.

"No. I am Greg, an EMT. I saw Dr. Paul Smith get his Land Rover nailed hard by a dual cab black pickup with bull bars that sped away. Dr. Smith will be fine. Is Kim, is she okay?

"Kim is okay and safe. I need you to describe what you meant by 'Land Rover nailed hard by a dual cab black pickup with bull bars', he asked.

"Well, to be honest, it looked like Dr. Paul Smith's Land Rover was hit deliberately on purpose. That truck took a direct aim at Dr. Smith's SUV. It sped away so fast around the curve I could not get the license plate information." Greg replied, curious that an 'agent from Homeland Security' had Kim's phone and he wondered about the entire situation. *Odd…yes…*

"Thank you. You have been a huge help. Thank you for the information as it is valuable. Have a good day. Goodbye," he ended the call.

Agent Thompson phoned Agent Woods who was headed to the Leawood home with his partner, Agent Knight. Plans had changed. The assassin was in Colorado and not far away!

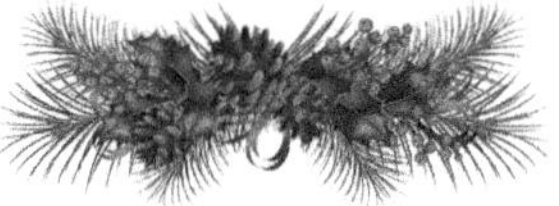

Recovered but shaky, Kim grabbed her phone from the agent and called her friend, Sarah Leawood, a nurse who worked in the emergency department of a level one trauma center in Lakewood, CO. Sarah and her husband, Aaron, an emergency room doctor at the same hospital, had planned to spend most of the day with their children, Danny age 12, and Lisa age 8, plus his mother, Alice, and housekeeper, Sadie, in Estes Park.

"Hi, Kim. What is up? We are about to head to Estes Park. The weather is nice, the elk are still in Estes Park and the lower areas of Rocky Mountain National Park (RMNP). Trail Ridge Road is now open in RMNP. As you know, Lisa turns nine tomorrow, and she wanted to go to Estes Park to celebrate."

"I am so deeply sorry, Sarah. Something is going on and I need all of you to come to my gallery in Evergreen, right now. You, Aaron, Danny, Lisa, Alice, and Sadie are to come here ASAP but drive safely. Be watchful…" Kim sobbed on the word 'watchful', and Agent Thompson grabbed her phone.

"Aaron, I think Kim is in trouble," Sarah handed her cell over to her husband.

"Kim, are you okay?" Aaron inquired.

"Dr. Aaron Leawood? This is Agent Thompson from Homeland Security. We have a situation and need all of you to come to the gallery in Evergreen right away. I mean all six of you, to the gallery, now. Questions will be answered upon your arrival." Agent Thompson directed.

"I don't understand, but we'll go up to Evergreen before heading to RMNP (Rocky Mountain National Park)." Aaron confirmed. Then both Sarah and Aaron watched as two armored SUVs pulled into the Leawood driveway.

Agent Woods introduced himself and Agent Knight to the family. Finding out Agent Thompson was on the phone with Aaron, he asked Aaron to hang up so he could call Agent Thompsom back.

Agent Woods and Agent Thompson had words and agreed that the plan would change to Plan B and he hung up. The agents knew their back up plans and would modify all plans at any given moment! That is how they were trained, to be the best at what they do. That is how the FBI (*Federal Bureau of Investigation*) worked.

"I am terribly sorry, but we have a situation and I need you to cooperate. I do not want to scare the children. You are to come with us immediately. I do not want to scare anyone at all, but it is imperative that you ALL come with us now, in our armored SUVs."

Aaron and Sarah were bewildered. "What is going on?" Sarah asked.

"Please, Mrs. Leawood, this will be much easier if you cooperate. The six of you need to split up and get into our armored SUVs now, for your safety. You and both children in one and Aaron, Alice, and Sadie in the other. Questions will be answered later," and Agent Woods directed the family into both vehicles.

Once inside the vehicles, Agent Woods told them that the situation had changed, thus they were now headed to the Denver Federal Center and to the offices of the FBI. Agent Knight informed his occupants of the same. No one was to ask questions until after they arrived at their destination.

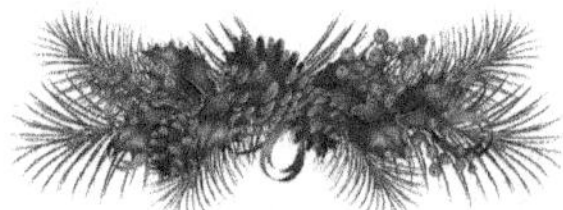

In Evergreen, Agents Thompsom and Hughes informed Kim, Nancy, and Richard, who had just arrived, that now they were on Plan B. Once safely ensconced inside the armored vehicles, they were informed that their destination was the Denver Federal Center, and all questions would be answered when they arrived.

Chapter Three

The agents coordinated together so they all arrived near the same time. With bewildered occupants, they drove through their assigned gate and to the building that housed the FBI (Federal Bureau of Investigation) and Homeland Security.

The Denver Federal Center, located in Lakewood, CO, has over 6,200 government employees. The area is large, to say the least, and currently has ninety buildings. The facility was home to offices, warehouses, labs, and special use space.

As such, there are twenty-eight different Federal agencies on-site, making it the largest concentration of Federal agencies outside of Washington, DC. A litany of government agencies was housed at the center, and the agents parked in front of the building that housed the FBI and Homeland Security.

Everyone exited the SUVs as instructed and followed the agents inside the building. They were met by the head of the Homeland Security in Denver, Director James Tilson.

Director Tilson informed them that they were completely safe, and that each person must go through a Federal Screening Process in the main lobby before entering the rest of the building.

One by one, the Leawood family, Alice, and Sadie, followed by Kim, Nancy, and Richard showed their identification, except for the children, Danny, and Lisa.

"Mom, this is like the airport except we don't have luggage!" Danny, aged twelve, with dark hair and eyes of cobalt blue yelled excitedly.

"Yes, Danny, and please don't yell." Sarah responded as she helped blonde haired and blue-eyed Lisa, aged eight going on 9 tomorrow, through the process.

Personal items were run through an x-ray machine, much like airport screenings, and each person walked through metal detectors. Of course, no weapons or incendiary devices were noted.

The group was escorted to a guard desk to be signed in, have their photo taken, and each was issued a visitor badge, to be always worn above the waist, and the badges stayed on each person while at the fed center. Aaron and Sarah helped the children secure their badges. All mobile phones were confiscated and would be returned when they were released from safety.

"I'm official," Danny proclaimed and grinned. "Just like the spy shows and NCIS on television!"

"Yes, Danny, you are, indeed," replied Director Tilson as he smiled down at the young boy, soon to be a teenager at 13 in a few more months.

"Now, we have one more step before going further. As required by federal COVID-19 safety protocols, each of you must wear a high-quality mask, for now, as Denver has an uptick of COVID-19 cases at this time." And they placed their masks on as directed.

"Follow me, please," and the masked visitors were taken to one of the conference rooms that the FBI used. "Have a seat, please. Water will be brought in shortly." Director Tilson informed the group. "You may all remove your masks now. You have been together long enough to have given each other germs or viruses."

Everyone found a nice and comfortable padded black leather chair to sit in at the large rectangular brown oak table. FBI emblems and government pictures adorned the walls, and the United States Flag was standing in one corner.

"This looks 'official', Dad." Danny whispered to Aaron.

"You got that right, Son," he replied as he smiled at Danny. Danny had finally started to call him "Dad" last Christmas, a major step for the young boy, who had been abused and traumatized by his biological father.

Aaron loved Danny as his own son, and had adopted him after he married Danny's mom, Sarah. Aaron was also happy that Danny's attention-deficit/hyperactivity disorder (ADHD) was better with the right medication.

Agents Thompson and Woods sat down near the group as did Director Tilson. "Before you ask questions, I want to inform you of why you are here." Director Tilson looked at each face in the room.

"You are completely safe," he continued as he chose his words carefully since the two children were present. "You are here because the handler that Steve Daily and Gary Moore worked for is now in Colorado. Furthermore, we now know that person is in this area."

His face serious, Director Tilson added, "This means you are not safe outside of this facility and campus. We have set up food and special temporary FBI living quarters in this building. Hopefully, things will wrap up quickly and you can get back to your normal lives as soon as possible. You may now ask questions."

Kim was on that fast with the first question. "How is my husband, Dr. Paul Smith? Is he safe? I must know right now!" Kim demanded as she glared at the director's face, and stared into his eyes, in a challenge, because Paul was her life.

"Mrs. Smith, your husband was taken to the level one trauma center directly west of where we are right now. You can see the facility through those windows." He pointed to the windows looking out towards the west. "At this time, he is in surgery for his broken right leg, and we can't let you go to the hospital." Director Tilson explained. "It's not safe for you to do so."

"I want to be there for my husband," Kim replied, and, as she looked over to Nancy and the others, as stoic as she could be, a lone tear ran down her cheek, and Agent Thompson handed her a tissue box.

"Not now, Mrs. Smith. The doctors, Dr. Russel Williams, and Dr. Thomas Caine will update you on his condition, and we have two agents, Agent Woodson, and Agent Mason protecting him. Your husband is safe, but you cannot join him just yet."

"Those two doctors are the best at what they do," Aaron informed Kim gently. "I personally know them. That is the hospital where Paul, Sarah, and I work."

Kim nodded her head in understanding as she knew that the assassin had tried to kill her husband and she trusted the doctors mending Paul's broken leg, and the agents protecting him.

Still, it was hard not to be at the hospital when one's husband was in surgery. Married just over five months and her heart wanted to be near Paul.

It hurt terribly to not be there for her husband, and guilt filled her with remorse that this was all her fault…it was all on her and her alone…if she had not moved to Evergreen…Paul would not be in surgery, everyone would be safe, but she would not have known the LOVE she shared with Paul…

"Sounds like you guys have everything covered," Nancy responded, and she looked around the room. "What are we supposed to do now? What is the next step?"

"Agent Hughes will take you to your quarters and nourishment will be provided. One guard will be posted outside your door. This is because you are in a highly classified building, in a just as highly classified building complex, and we cannot have any of you walking around and looking in places where civilians are not allowed. Do not leave your quarters unless an agent picks you up. Do you all understand?"

After they nodded in the affirmative, Director Tilson continued, "Agent Hughes will take you to your quarters now. I will update you when new intelligence is received and proven."

The group followed Agent Hughes down a hall to an elevator that took them down two floors. Once out of the elevator, he escorted them to Barrack 16. Barrack 16 was part of the building they were in and located on basement level two.

"You have two basements here? Wow," Danny remarked.

"Actually, we have more than 32 different below ground levels, or basements, that I know of." Agent Hughes replied. The entire group was awestruck and wordless upon hearing that comment! "I cannot tell you everything, but I can say we have ice core samples and other samples stored here at this complex. I can only tell you what we are allowed to tell tour groups when they come through."

Once inside Barrack 16, Agent Hughes explained the food delivery and how Barrack 16 was laid out.

"You will receive three meals a day, along with snacks and bottled water, and you have a large refrigerator and cooking range with a micro-wave to use," he explained. "The kitchen cabinets are stocked with basic pantry items along with fresh bread, and fresh milk, eggs, cheeses, and fruit are in the refrigerator now, stocked today as we drove to the fed center."

Agent Hughes smiled at the children before he continued, "Any medical needs or medicine will be taken care of by our physicians on base. We do not have clothing for you, but we do have military style pants and t-shirts, and some military style scrubs."

"Three meals a day? How long are we going to be here?" Aaron asked gruffly. "I'm an ER (emergency room) doctor and I'm needed at the hospital next door!"

"Dr. Leawood, you and your entire group are our top priority, and our job is to keep you protected for the duration of this assignment. This is the safest place to be right now, especially since you are a large group. Understood?" Agent Hughes asked.

"That could be one day or two weeks." Agent Hughes stated in a matter-of-fact tone. "You are here because all of you are targeted by a crazed and unpredictable assassin, and here you will remain for now. I have my orders." The group nodded in agreement.

"As I speak, agents are closing in on the assassin – the expert one who eliminated two people in Boston last night, tried to eliminate Dr. Paul Smith today, and has plans on the elimination of others. Once we have that taken care of, you will all be free to go." Agent Hughes looked at each member of the group.

"Now, this quarter has four bedrooms, two on either side of the main living room space that opens to the dining and kitchen areas. Each bedroom contains four single beds. Singles, no doubles or king size. This is military housing so you each have your own bed since there are sixteen single beds and nine of you."

Lisa started crying and Sarah wrapped her arms around the little girl in comfort. "What's wrong, Lisa? Are you scared? Everything will be okay, I promise."

"No, I am not scared. This is like an adventure." More tears welled up in her blue eyes and flowed down her face.

"Then why are you crying?" Sarah asked in a soothing voice as she rubbed Lisa's back in comfort.

"My birthday! No birthday for me tomorrow. I do not get to have birthday presents or a cake or anything," she wailed and threw herself into Aaron's strong arms.

"Honey, you will still have your birthday and your presents, on another day. You will be nine tomorrow and we will sing, talk, and play. After this adventure, the big birthday celebration will start. Okay, Honey?" Aaron asked his daughter.

Lisa nodded yes, she hiccupped, and wiped at her tears with tissues given to her by Kim.

Agent Hughes then left them in the main living room, and everyone sat down on chairs or sofas. They had music, games, and a large flat screen television, but they could not get on the internet. They had a computer to play pre-installed games, but no access to the outside.

Soon, a late lunch was provided to the group, and it arrived with a chocolate cake with the number 9 written on the top. No candles, but Lisa grinned happily when she saw that she had a birthday cake one day before her birthday!

Director Tilson hung up his phone and shook his head. He should have been notified sooner. The Boston detectives were slow on this one. The news report and new intelligence would not go over well with Kim and Nancy. They had to know, though, so he went down to Barrack 16, and knocked on the door.

"Come in," Aaron welcomed the director after he opened the door. "Care to sit in the main living area with us?"

Director Tilson sighed and then he sat down near Kim and Nancy. Both Danny and Lisa were playing a board game and the sugar rush from the chocolate cake consumed them, and neither child looked up as the Director entered the barracks. *Yet Danny did see, and he listened…*

"I have news to impart, and I need you to remain as calm as possible. It is best we do not frighten the children. Gather around closer to me. I will state facts as I know them and please do not take it wrong and think that I do not care. I do care. I care a great deal. As military, facts are what I deliver."

"What has happened now? Is it Paul? What has happened?" Kim whispered in sheer terror, trembling to get her words out of her mouth.

"Your husband is fine, and he is safe. Do not worry about him. All of you are connected in one way or another and are perfectly safe in this building and in this bunker," he voiced to Kim in a low tone.

"Please do not worry about your husband. He is fine and has the best of care right now. We went so far to vet the nurse and surgeons. The staff are aware and will alert us with hand signals if a person of suspicion is present or comes anywhere near your husband."

After a glance back at the kids still at rambunctious play with the board game, he announced that more intelligence had come in. "I am terribly sorry to have to give you more sad news. Kim and Nancy, please try to remain calm. This news affects both of you more than the others, and most especially you, Kim. I am so terribly sorry."

Nancy wrapped her arms around Kim and Sarah went and wrapped her arms around both women.

After looking to see what the kids were doing, he continued.

"Kim, your ex-housekeeper in Boston, and your ex-gardener, the two that had married and bought your homes, were found dead this morning when a couple staying at their Airbnb couldn't locate them," the director whispered, then glanced at the children again before he continued.

"They were taken out hit style, bullets to the head while they slept, no pain, a silencer was used, and a note was found. The note read, 'Four down, ten to go', and now we know this assassin is deranged. Assassins have a MO (modus operandi) of taking out certain targets, they do not make plans for the number of, or the specific people this assassin has planned, as you are innocent. This means he or she has a vendetta and he or she is mentally unstable, and that makes this situation much more dangerous. The ten to go are all of you, I am sure of that."

Kim stood up, whirled around, and ran into the bathroom on one side of the barracks. Nancy followed her with Sarah not far behind.

"It is my fault! I am the one to blame. If I had not married Steve none of this would have happened. It is not right! Look how many people I have killed. That is four already, and Paul was almost killed!"

Huge sobs ripped through Kim's body as she broke down and slid down the wall to the floor with her back. "That hurt! All I need to do now is make my back worse."

"No, Kim. Your back will remain fine as 'Nurse Nancy' is on it. Relax a bit, let the nerve stimulator wires trigger so your back pain goes away – for the most part." Nancy worried that Kim might damage herself and not know until it was too late.

"Your back will be fine, Kim. You simply landed your tailbone on a hard surface." Sarah tried to soothe her friend.

"It is not your fault, Kim. This madman is deranged and dangerous. You did not make him that way." Sarah rationalized to Kim. "Now, please dry your tears and blow your nose. We must get back out with the others before the children notice we are gone, and they get upset. Put a smile on your countenance, a pretend smile for the children."

Sarah went back out to the group with a smile on her face. A short time later, both Kim and Nancy emerged together and smiled at each other as if sharing a joke, just for the kids in case they saw them come back out.

"I will keep you apprised of the situation, and I will let myself out the door," the director responded. "All of you are doing well given the circumstances. Try to read or watch a movie. I will take my leave now."

Nancy and Richard huddled together on a sofa lost in thought…or at least Nancy was lost in thought.

Richard is the best thing to ever happen in my life…and I am so giddy with his love for me…what would I do without him…warmth and electricity flowed throughout her body and blood…yet she thought about never wanting to lose him…

Chapter Four

As soon as Paul arrived in the busy ER, one of the ER doctors temporarily took over his care and ordered a large bore (18 gauge) IV (intra-venous catheter) placed and normal saline started. Paul was given Fentanyl IV for his pain after he signed papers for surgery and two orthopedic doctors, Dr. Russell Williams, and Dr. Thomas Caine, were in the ER and waiting for his arrival.

Dr. Williams and Dr. Caine took over Paul's case after the IV was established, labs drawn, especially for a type and cross match as blood would be needed, IV meds for pain and a strong IV antibiotic infused.

A CT (computerized tomography scan) of Paul's head and neck was done to check for any issues (top priority), and none were noted. An X-ray imaging followed of his right leg (to see all the breaks and how they needed to be aligned for use during surgery). Those steps done; Paul was whisked away to an operating room.

After Paul was transferred to the OR table, the anesthesiologist immediately placed Paul under, and he was asleep.

Two orthopedic surgeons, Dr. Williams, and Dr. Caine, worked in tandem to fix the compound break. His leg had been prepped and sterile drapes placed. Everyone was in place and knew their jobs!

The wound was irrigated with normal saline solution, to help remove debris. Then the leg was irrigated with an antibiotic solution of cefazolin before beginning the surgery. Agents Woodson and Mason stood guard outside the operating room.

Paul's bones were moved back into a regular and more normal position to reduce the fracture.

The surgeons discussed the best way to move forward in Paul's case, and decided on pins, plates, and screws to aid in the mending of his leg. A cast would be applied once the hardware was in place, secured, the wound stitched closed, and the leg looked as expected on the post operative X-ray.

The surgery was successful and after 30 minutes in the post operative room, Paul was transferred to Room 316, a private room on the orthopedic floor, and his two guards from Homeland Security had followed Paul to each of his stops, radiology, surgery, and the third floor as they knew their jobs, too.

Healing was just starting as new bone tissue was created during the mending process. This was a three-stage process, and the surgeons reminded Paul of the stages once he was in Room 316 and stabilized in the bed. Inflammation. Repair. Remodeling. Paul was in the Inflammation stage.

Paperwork and handouts were left with Paul after the mandatory teaching was completed. As a doctor, Paul knew the stages, as surgeons they had to do their teaching.

Paul listened to the surgeons' ramble regarding the swelling and redness (inflammation) due to increased blood flow in the area. Paul was drowsy and he wanted them to sum it up fast. He needed to know about Kim and the others.

"The bone will be kept still (immobilized) in a cast. It is vital that your broken bones do not move while they heal. Your body will create new bone tissue during this stage, Paul." Dr Williams continued. "It's too soon to know how long your cast will be on."

Paul nodded in agreement and Dr. Williams continued, "The remodeling stage can take months as your bone gets stronger, grows thicker, and calcifies." The surgeons took their leave then so a registered nurse, Pam, could take over.

"Good afternoon, Dr. Smith. I am Pam, your nurse. Can I get you anything?"

"Hi, Pam. Ice chips? My mouth is dry, and I want to talk with the two guards outside my door." Paul responded.

"I brought ice chips in with me, Dr. Smith. I need to do a quick assessment of the blood flow to both feet, set you up with a pain pump, and show you the button to push for more pain medicine when you need it."

As she spoke, she checked his pedal (foot) pulse and capillary refill time informing him of her findings which were expected. "Your leg must remain elevated for now and the surgeons will let you know when that will end, and I have one injection for you, in your stomach."

"I know the medication so give me the injection, I don't want to get a blood clot," Paul responded. "Can one of the guards come in now?"

"Sure, Dr. Smith. We have plenty of time to go over your cast care and physical therapy as you will be here for a while. I will get a guard for you now, this button is your call light; if you need anything push the button, okay?" Pam looked at Paul for confirmation and he nodded yes.

"This button is for your pain medicine, your PCA (patient-controlled analgesia) machine. As you know, with a PCA you do not need to wait for a nurse to get pain relief and you cannot overdose as the pump will not allow that to happen with its pre-programming, and the pump is locked." Pam glanced at her patient.

Paul nodded yes and closed his eyes praying that Kim and the rest were safe and okay.

Agent Mason came into the room and left Agent Woodson at the door. "Hello, Dr. Smith. I am Agent Mason. I know you are worried about your wife and the others. They are safe and are in a barracks at the Denver Federal Center."

"Really? The fed center just east of us, of my hospital, my hospital room? Why are they there and was anyone hurt? I need to know now." Paul looked directly into Agent Mason's eyes.

"No one was hurt, and they are fine. We changed plans to Plan B after intelligence informed us that two other people were taken out hit-style early this morning in Boston, namely your wife's ex housekeeper and gardener. I am sorry to be the one to tell you this news." Agent Mason had concern written all over his face.

"We now know that your motor vehicle accident was deliberate and intentional, the assassin tried to take you out, and they failed. The Director of the Homeland Security in Denver, decided that keeping everyone secure at the fed center was the safest and easiest way to protect them."

"Can I talk to my wife? Can I call her, please?" Paul needed to hear Kim's voice, he had to hear her voice.

'I will let you know when you can talk with her, okay? It should not be too long, now that your surgery is over, and everyone is safe. Try to rest a bit, Dr. Smith. I will go back out and talk with the director now." With that, Agent Mason left the room.

Paul closed his eyes and fell asleep.

Paul awoke with a start. What is going on now? He could hear yelling in the hallway outside his room. Then a single gunshot and suddenly all was quiet before voices came to him from outside his door, one loaded with anger.

The assassin must be here and outside my door…fear gripped him immediately…I can't move or find safety…nowhere to go, I'm immobile…maybe they don't know my room number…best to keep listening for any signs of someone at the door to my room… all I have is a single plastic spoon in my ice chips…not good for self-defense…

Agent Mason came into my room, and he looked a bit disheveled. "Everything is okay, Dr. Smith. The assassin was here, still is here, but *not* eliminated; captured and tied down, yes. He was caught wearing surgical scrubs and a white lab coat he had stolen from the doctor's changing room. I wounded him but he is alive, wounded so that the FBI and Homeland Security can ask questions. We must make sure that he was and is working alone. Had he had time to try and aim for a kill shot, I would have killed him."

"How…where…?" Paul was confused. "Is that him yelling in anger that I hear? Is he American? I hear more than one language. That is a Russian accent! Is Russia involved in this insane situation?"

"You are perceptive. We caught him headed to the door of your room; he wore no credentials. Your nurse, Pam, alerted us with silent hand motions that he was not on staff. He reached for a gun, and I wounded him. You are safe and you will remain that way. We vetted your care givers and nurse, and taught hand signals if something was not right. Pam did her job." Agent Mason replied with a smile.

"You have a guardian angel looking out for you today. Twice in one day and both failed attempts. I will not bore you with the rest, but Agent Woodson and I will remain in place, for now. Excuse me, please, I must go back out and deal with business."

Agent Mason alerted Director Tilson to what had occurred at the hospital, and that additional agents were taking the assassin to Washington, DC, for wound care and interrogation. It was imperative to find out if he had acted alone or not.

Director Tilson informed Kim and the rest of the group that the assassin was caught and in the process of arrival in Washington, DC, for interrogation.

"It is over. Truly? I can go to Paul now?" Kim tossed out a barrage of questions as she stared into Director Tilson's eyes.

"First, Kim, your husband is okay. He is eating ice chips and napping. I am sorry to say that you cannot see him just yet."

"Why not?" Kim demanded angrily. She needed to be with her husband, with Paul. "You have the perpetrator!!!" She stated in a harsh and accusatory tone of voice.

Nancy wrapped her arms around Kim, and asked the director to finish what he came to say.

Dr. Leawood suggested that everyone take a deep breath; then let it out slowly. He aimed to calm the group down. A lot had happened in just a few hours, and they needed to regain control of their emotions, if that was even possible.

"Kim, and all of you, the assassin is enroute to DC on a military plane with a military doctor and nurse tending to his wounds. Once the interrogation is over, and we know for sure that he acted alone, you will all be released." Director Tilson smiled at the group.

"I expect you will leave here early in the morning. The agents will take you back to where they picked you up, except for Kim. You will have an escort to your husband's hospital room. I must go now. Try to get some rest tonight. You are all exhausted. It has been a long day for all of us. Rest the best you can. Goodnight and see you in the morning."

Chapter Five

Agents Mason and Woodson guarded the assassin, 'Jeffrey Sanders', while Homeland Security landed a military helicopter on the hospital helicopter pad. Agent Mason remained at Dr Smith's door and kept him under guard.

Jeffrey Sanders was taken by gurney and under heavy guard to the chopper and the chopper flew directly to Denver International Airport. The chopper landed near a military plane, and the assassin was moved onto the plane that would head for DC.

In flight, a military doctor and nurse cared for his gunshot wound in his left shoulder area.

Unfortunately, no fingerprints could be obtained as the assassin had used acid on his fingertips negating the ability to obtain his prints. No matter, they would heal in a month or so and prints would be obtained then, using the international fingerprint database known as AFIS (Automated Fingerprint Identification System).

Upon arrival in DC, the assassin was taken to the FBI's complex and remained under high security, strapped down on a gurney, and taken inside to a large interrogation room.

"I tell you nothing! Ничего нет, я говорю тебе, совсем ничего. Nothing!" the assassin yelled out in a mix of English and Russian.

The rest of the interrogation included Interpol, and the Director of the CIA, Richard Cook. He answered directly to the Director of National Intelligence.

"I say nothing!!" Jeffrey Sanders yelled out again, his face a purplish red from his vocal outbursts. Then utter silence…as he stopped breathing. Unfortunately, no further intelligence would be obtained from him. *He was gone…just like that…*

Upon autopsy, the medical examiner found that the assassin had suffered a massive coronary. No chance for his fingertips to regenerate and obtain prints. All they had was "Jeffrey Sanders" and that was an alias since he was Russian.

Homeland Security took over responsibility of the body of the assassin and Richard Cook reported detailed intelligence to the President directly, and to Director Tilson at the Denver Federal Center. The President was safe and would remain safe as he had more security than any other person on the planet. He was never a true concern.

They wanted intelligence, the reason he was in the USA, and that would not happen now. But the assassin was after intelligence of some kind that the USA had, and that was a puzzle, for now. Hopefully a lead would come their way and that intel can be ascertained for what it is and how to secure it, yet for now, they were at a dead stop.

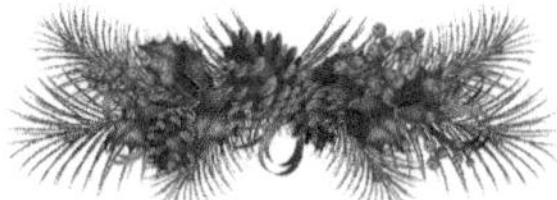

Director Tilson took the information update, and then went down to Kim and the group.

"I have a new intel update although I did not expect to be back here this evening. Jeffrey Sanders, not his real name as we now know he was Russian, died of a heart attack before he could be interrogated in DC." He looked at the group he had been treating like family, but military style. In the span of a few hours, they had become real family to him. Blood does not make a family.

The love he saw from afar made his heart feel lost; he needed to find the right woman…but what woman would want a 50-year-old military man with odd hours and short cropped hair…a man who could not divulge top-secret information to… what would they talk about…hmmm…

"We can leave now, correct?" Dr. Leawood asked in an expectant tone of voice.

"No, Dr. Leawood. I am sorry, but to be extra safe you will remain here overnight, and then leave in the morning. This will ensure that no one else is a target, and that, most likely, no one else was working with the perpetrator, at least not stateside."

"Thank you, Director Tilson, for going above and beyond, for everything," Sarah replied. "You and your men are amazing." You all work together as a perfect team and are highly skilled and trained. I am in awe of you."

"We all are. Saying thank you is not enough. I mean, that is all we can say, but know that we are completely grateful." Dr. Leawood agreed. Danny and Lisa smiled as they knew things were okay now, and they had decided to make a fort of sorts with extra blankets in the room they would sleep in tonight, playing spies for the good guys. Children can be quite creative when electronic devices are taken away from their hands now and then.

Director Tilson left after smiling at both children. Finally, after such a dreadful and fast paced day, they could relax. Tomorrow would be a new day, a birthday day for Lisa, a healing and loving day for the families, a day for Kim to reunite with her husband, and a day to give thanks to Jesus for keeping them safe.

PART 2

Chapter Six

Nancy and Richard were snuggled up on the couch, yet not watching the movie on her large flat screen television. Balsam scented candles burned above the fireplace that was not in use; the glow gave a soft light to the room. Both were lost in thought, thinking about the events they had been through the last week.

Nancy's two floor, three bed, three bath, log and river rock home on highway 74, a short drive west of Kim and Paul's condominium, in the Heart of Evergreen, was comforting with a homey feel throughout – a woman's touch.

Richard was at Nancy's home more often than his own since the assassin showed up and he wanted to turn their relationship into a permanent one. *Was Nancy ready…I pray she is because I am ready, and I refuse to let her get away…*

"We did it, we survived, and we are stronger for it, Nancy. I could not appreciate the fear you felt back in Boston, and now I do. At least in part." Richard kissed her forehead.

"Actually, what I had felt back in my former life in Boston was nothing compared to the last couple of days." Nancy looked up at Richard.

"I did not experience what Kim did, with two assassins on her butt, and Kim literally running for her life." She let out a deep sigh of relief once again and thanked Jesus for getting them through the ordeal.

"And I never want to feel how scared Kim was during her ordeal in Boston. Remember, I found out about it after she had fled to Hartford, CT."

"I have been thinking, Nancy, and I know one thing for sure. I do not want to lose you, ever." Richard gave her a sweet and deep kiss, then continued.

"I don't like being apart from you, living separately, this ordeal has taught me that you are the most precious person in my life," he whispered in her ear before he breathed on it in a sensual manner.

"Oh…that was nice, do that again to my ear please. Wait. What? What are you saying? Do you want to move into my home with me?" Nancy was unsure about that idea. Yet she loved Richard and did not want to ever lose him.

"Well, yes, no, well yes, but not like that. You really have my tongue wrapped and tumbling around, woman!" He laughed loudly and Nancy giggled, then both broke out laughing with tears. Laughing was good for the soul and it had been too long since they had had a good laugh.

"Seriously, Nancy, I do want us to live together, as soon as possible, but not exactly in that way. I want and need more than that." Richard turned around and stared into Nancy's blue eyes while he pulled a small blue velvet ring box out of his pocket, and popped it open, facing Nancy.

"Will you marry me, Nancy? Will you be my wife, my partner, forever and ever? Will you let me love you for the rest of my life?"

Nancy could read the honest and real love in Richard's eyes. She was lost in his beautiful blue orbs. Time stood still for her. She was mesmerized by those gorgeous eyes. *My hopes and dreams… mine…forever…*

"Earth to Nancy. Are you okay?" Richard asked, perplexed at her non-response, and not sure she would say yes to his proposal.

"Yes, Richard. Yes, I will marry you and yes, I am okay." Nancy cracked up laughing and told him she had been lost in his gorgeous eyes and how much she loved him back; how much she needed him to be with her always.

"Dude, for what are you waiting? I want to see that ring on my finger! I promise to be good and not get lost in it," she giggled.

Richard smiled as he took the two-carat cushion cut diamond in a cathedral setting engagement ring out of the blue velvet cushion box and slid it on her left ring finger. Nancy's hand had never looked better. Smaller diamonds arched up to the center stone all set in yellow gold with white gold prongs.

"It's beautiful, Richard, and it fits perfectly." Nancy smothered Richard with a happy and loving kiss. "I love you so much! I love you to the moon and back a thousand times!"

"You've made me the happiest man in the world." With a remote in hand, Richard turned the television off, then lifted Nancy up and into his strong mountain man arms, he blew out the candles, and strode with purpose into her (soon their) master bedroom with ensuite.

Tonight was their night, and theirs alone. No one else existed in the world. Everything felt perfect. Safe in each other's arms, nestled together, in love, and loving each other as only a man and woman can do.

Tomorrow would come soon enough...and with that, work at the gallery for Nancy, and Richard was in the middle of carving a bedroom set for a client...

Chapter Seven

K im sat at Paul's bedside in his hospital room. They were holding hands and discussing events during the previous week.

"Some of that day is still hard to wrap my head around, Paul murmured. "I cannot believe I was almost taken out by that hit man twice in one day. I love you so very much, Kim."

Kim stood up and bent over to her husband's ear and whispered, "I love you, too." She gave Paul a sweet and tender kiss as his nurse, Pam, walked into the room.

"Great to see you feeling better Dr. Smith. If you did not have a wounded leg, I would tell you both to get a room!" Pam snickered and they all laughed.

"Physical therapy will be here soon. Would you like a pain pill before they start? As you know, initial physical therapy after surgery is painful, and the medicine will help."

"That would be wonderful, Pam. Thank you. I am happy to be past the stage of needing that PCA pump." He grinned at his nurse and then went back to sweet and tender kisses with his wife.

Paul and Kim had received the teaching and paperwork related to all the teaching done all week. Paul's recovery could be up to six months. So far, he was on schedule as his x-rays showed healing had begun and new bone growth noted.

Paul was thankful that his nerves and blood vessels had not received too much damage. He knew crutches were his new friend, and mobility teaching had been, and continued to be taught to both.

Paul was a model patient in doing his physiotherapy, and he wanted to regain muscle strength, movement, and flexibility. He knew certain exercises must be done before and after his cast was removed.

He would miss driving for at least nine weeks, or longer, and being out on the ER floor. Paul almost forgot that he would require a new SUV since his was totaled in that ravine.

Once the cast was off, his rehabilitation exercises had restored normal strength and movement in his leg, and he regained lost muscle mass, he would be able to be on the ER floor once again, partially limited depending on what stage of healing the x-rays showed.

Discharge day arrived and Paul was glad. He would miss the staff who cared for him, but he would be back home with Kim soon – as she drove them both to their condominium. More teaching had been done, and he had his follow-up appointments scheduled so things were looking up. At age 38, his bones would heal fast, but not as fast if he had been younger.

"We are home, Paul. I will help you out and you can use your crutches to get to the elevator." Kim assisted Paul in standing and he 'crutched' his way to their elevator.

Both were thankful that their condominium had a personal elevator from the basement and garage space up to each floor of the condominium. Kim had bought the condominium because of her back pain and now that the elevator would help Paul as well.

"Does your recliner feel better than your hospital bed?" Kim queried as she kissed Paul on the top of his head.

"Oh, yes, but I'm looking forward to my personal no-get-the-cast-wet-bath you'll help me with every single day!" He gave Kim a wink and raised his eyebrow in a grin.

"I see what is coming, and you are going to milk this situation for all you can," she squealed as he lightly squeezed her butt. *Her heart shaped butt...the one he had missed...the one he would sleep next to tonight...*

Chapter Eight

Sarah was concerned about Danny and Lisa. As a registered nurse, she knew that the trauma of the events the week before could have lifelong effects on one or both children. Sarah watched for signs that would indicate they had problems.

Lisa appeared happy, but then they had gone to Estes Park and celebrated her birthday and turning age nine. So far, Lisa did not exhibit anxiety or fear, her concentration remained normal, and she slept all night long; except for their first night back at home and Lisa woke up screaming from a nightmare.

Surprisingly, it was Danny who helped Lisa out the most. Both Aaron and Sarah reassured Lisa, and they supported Lisa. Danny hit the nail on the head and he and Lisa were closer than ever before as siblings.

Danny assured Lisa that first week that no one was coming after them, and that no one could hurt them. Danny used a spy game that he created in his one brain, to help Lisa and it worked. Kids can be highly creative, and Danny was no exception, despite his ADHD.

No doubt, the spy game helped Danny out as well. Danny was angry the first day after leaving the bunker, but not for long. He had worked out his anger talking with Aaron and, at almost thirteen, he succeeded.

Danny was no longer angry about the hit man and what he had done; he was not happy about it, but his anger at that man was gone – in past tense. Aaron had helped him; dad had helped him. Dad. Danny accepted Aaron as his real dad now and had since right before last Christmas.

Danny understood what happened, all of it, and even in the bunker he was listening in when the adults thought he was only playing with Lisa. Danny was able to talk about all the events and what the assassin did with his mom and dad when Lisa was otherwise occupied or asleep.

Instead of being withdrawn, or issues with interrupted sleep patterns, or even a need to be alone, Danny was closer than ever to his sister and parents. He did not cling to fear, he lived life, and that meant doing things with his friends and family, and scouting. Danny was growing up fast.

After taking a week off to be with both children, Sarah went back to work in the busy ER. Aaron did the same. They knew that Grandma Alice and Sadie were with the kids, and with summer vacation from school in full swing, both had activities to keep them busy.

As for Alice, she was fine and life was back to normal for her, partly because she had been terrified of her own abusive daughter back in Colorado Springs; now she had gone through both events, and she had won. Sadie preferred to talk about bits and pieces of that week with her best friend, Alice, and that bonded the women closer than ever.

Nancy swept into the art gallery and both Kim and Paul looked up to see her smile and take light steps as she made her way toward the cash register and the diary of gallery events coming up.

"What gives?" Kim asked. "You are practically dancing around this morning. You did something! You are positively glowing!"

"I agree with Kim. You have anything juicy to tell us?" Paul asked in a joking manner. He was in a chair with his cast propped up as he was reading a medical journal.

"Nothing, Kim. It is June and I am happy to be back at work. Oh, and Richard will here later this morning as he has carved wood pieces at home that he wants to sell." Nancy hummed a soft tune.

"Yeah, you are not spilling the beans, Nancy! Richard is selling off carved wood pieces from his home. Why? Doesn't he require furniture? Also, you are practically singing this morning. Spill the beans and make them snappy my friend. I swear you have a new glow about you." Kim demanded to know what the gig was and then she saw it!

"You are engaged! Let me see that ring! Please?" Kim gushed with supreme happiness and a gleam in her eyes.

Nancy complied and showed Kim the ring under the light of the sunshine coming into the gallery from the east windows.

"It's beautiful and so are you, Nancy." Kim smiled at her best friend and then gave her a huge hug. "I'm so happy for you!"

Nancy walked over to Paul and showed him her ring. "It is beautiful. Congratulations! I had a feeling this was going to happen soon. Gut instinct," he winked back at her. "Or maybe, Richard and I had a man talk."

"You didn't tell me, Paul, and I'm your wife." Kim frowned in mock horror then kissed her husband on the cheek.

"Have you set a date yet? Fall or winter wedding? I need details!"

Kim was thrilled for Nancy as she had found true love in Evergreen just like Kim had found Paul.

"Saturday, July 25th. That is the date. A summer wedding that…" Kim interrupted her.

"Is that date solid? Only eight weeks to arrange a wedding and you know many people will want to be a part of it. Sarah and I will help you! A lovely late July wedding in the Heart of Evergreen. Did you secure the Lake House as a venue?" Kim was not letting Nancy get one single word in, and she grinned from ear to ear.

"Yes, the date is solid, and yes, I secured the Lake House for our venue. As for people, we only want our closest family and friends – no big wedding. We want a 'Nancy and Richard' style wedding. No white dress and veil or tuxedos. Truly, we just want a simple but tasteful wedding." Nancy grinned at Kim, and she smiled back before giving Nancy a warm-hearted hug!

"Oh. An intimate wedding with candles and fairy lights. So romantic." Kim thought back to last December and her own small and intimate winter wedding at the gallery of all places.

"The Lake House is lovely any time of the year," Paul remarked. "Plus, I can get in and out easy with my crutches. What else have you two decided?"

"We decided to live in my house, and Richard plans to sell his as we don't need it." Nancy informed Paul as Richard walked through the door with a carved wooden chest.

"Congratulations!" Kim and Paul spoke in unison, then laughed.

"Did you tell them already? You did not wait for me?" Richard shook his head at Nancy and smiled.

"Nope. Kim saw 'it' with the 'it' being the gorgeous ring you gave me. They could tell something was happening." Nancy gave Richard a peck on his lips. "I love you!"

"What are you planning to do, Richard? I have room for more pieces of carved furniture. Don't you want to keep some of it?" Kim peeped at Richard with a questioning look on her face.

"To be honest, I do not want to be away from Nancy any longer. The last week or so taught us all how fragile life can be. So, I am moving my favorite pieces into Nancy's house and the rest I am selling." Richard shared as he placed the chest into position.

"We have decided to be together 24/7 as of last night. I must admit that I feel safer in Richard's arms when I sleep now." Nancy blushed in a perky manner as she turned her gaze away.

"That's not all Richard's arms are good for!" Kim snickered, then broke out in a laugh which caused the other three to laugh.

"We plan to sell my house and, as you know, it is quite nice and well maintained." Richard continued, "I plan to ask 1.6 million for it, and it's worth that and a bit more."

'Dr. Paul', as he was affectionately nicknamed by the Leawood children, and Kim thought that made perfect sense.

"Good luck and may it sell quickly. Prices are at a premium in the real estate market right now." Paul glanced over to Richard, then continued, "Do you have a plan to promote the sale? Can we help?"

"I have a realtor already and she is taking care of all the details," Richard answered. "I can concentrate on my wood creations, and Nancy."

"Nice," Paul agreed as he changed the position of his leg with the cast still on it.

The follow up doctor visits and x-rays proved mending and healing were on schedule and physical therapy was going well. Paul made sure not to overdo anything, especially with Kim riding his butt if he tried to do anything she was against.

Leave it to Kim to be the 'Nurse Ratched' at home and at the gallery…Kim was not that bad…she simply wanted his leg to heal properly and so did he…

Soon Kim and Nancy were looking at the recent paintings that Richard would help hang on the gallery walls. "Do you want any of your mom's paintings to be displayed only – not for sale?" Nancy wondered aloud.

Mom…I miss mom and dad so much…Donald and Emma Pleasance had been killed in a one vehicle automobile accident right after her wedding to Steve – the assassin that tried to kill her…Dad was a careful driver, and the roads were not icy or wet…dry roads in September and not late at night…no skid marks…no clue as to why they went over the edge and into a ravine…they died on impact…with everything that's happened since then, Kim thought they could have been 'taken out' for some reason…Donald had been a retired history professor and Emma a shining light of beauty in the art world…she painted quality landscapes and seascapes…they'd just arrived back in Boston two weeks before, after a successful three-week art showing in London…

"Kim? Are you okay?" Nancy hugged her best friend. "I'm sorry I upset you."

"I am fine, truly. Great idea. I would like to see some of mom's pieces in the gallery with 'not for sale' signs on them. A bit of mom and dad would be here in Evergreen at our condominium and the gallery." Kim smiled back at Nancy. "We'll go over those pieces next week, okay?"

"You bet," Nancy said as she showed Richard where to hang a new painting, created by a local artist.

Kim's gallery was for not only her own pieces of art, but artworks from locals, and not only paintings. Inside glass cases smaller carved figurines of various materials, nativities, handmade quality jewelry with genuine gemstones, and other types of art were shown with special lighting.

Evergreen had an abundance of artists, an enclave of artistic and creative people who loved the Heart of Evergreen.

And art was her world, outside of Paul…laid back…artistic…scenic…and she had Paul…and Nancy and Richard…and the Leawood family…but SHE had PAUL…her love…their love…

Chapter Nine

Kim had just hung one of her mom's smaller pieces above the cash register on a north wall, when a customer walked in.

The gentleman introduced himself as Dmitry Ivanov, he spoke with a Russian accent, handed Kim his Denver business card, explained that he was an art collector, and that he lived in Denver. He hoped to eventually purchase a second home in the Evergreen area as he loved the feel and ambiance.

"Welcome to 'The Gallery Loft of Evergreen'," Kim welcomed the gentleman, who was dressed in extremely high-end business wear.

Yes…you are loaded…that Bentley you parked was not cheap…heck, you have a seven hundred million super yacht for all I know…a super-rich Russian…must be nice…

They shook hands and Kim noticed high-end jewelry on his wrists and fingers, as well as an Avant-Garde watch made of yellow gold featuring a smooth emerald gemstone face with yellow gold numbering beneath the crystal surface, surrounded by small round emeralds.

The man was obviously an extremely wealthy person, and he had no problem flaunting his wealth.

Flaunting what he wore without a personal bodyguard was dangerous…but he does not need a bodyguard…he is his own bodyguard…I wonder if he carries a gun…oh well…not my problem…I will just keep my eye on Mr. Rich Russian… and let him buy all the items he wants…

Evergreen was home for those who wanted the mountain scenery and lake, and many were members of the upper echelon in wealth with resources most do not have. They lived in the Heart of Evergreen or in wealthy areas of Genessee, next to Evergreen on the north side.

Mr. Ivanov wore his dark hair neatly trimmed as was his beard and mustache. Dark eyes smiled back at her. "Thank you, and please call me, Dmitry." Then he began to peruse the art hanging on the walls.

Nancy walked in with a small carved statue of Jesus created in jade by a local artist. She greeted Kim good morning and was introduced to Mr. Ivanov.

With a smile, he asked to be called, 'Dmitry' and she agreed before placing the hand carved statue inside a glass case with a card containing the artist's information and price. Afterwards, she added the piece to the gallery logbook – a digital document listing each piece in the gallery, the artist, and the asking price.

Dmitry soon found a piece that had been painted by Kim's mom, Emma. "I like this one very much. Why not sale it?" Dmitry enquired. "It is lovely, and the frame is unusual. I look for unique pieces."

"Since my mom died, I've wanted to keep her art and vision around me, both here and at home." Kim responded as she looked at the painting in question. "My heart would break if I sold this piece. I just cannot sell it."

"I am so sorry you lost your mom and I understand wanting to keep her work around you. Such nobleness and honesty are refreshing to hear. Many have no respect for their parents," Dmitry gave Kim a look of sincere and deep condolence before browsing other paintings and works of art.

Wow Kim thought…was this dude for real…really…was he really that kind and nice…who talks that way…I suppose Russian oligarchs might…maybe he does have a 700 million super yacht…I wonder if he will buy anything…his kindness and sincerity looked totally genuine…who knows how those rich Russian types are…I guess one must be one and/or around others who are to actually know…and here comes Richard…

Richard walked in with the last wooden piece that he wanted to sell, a lovely and partly art deco designed, hand carved coffee table that gleamed in the sunlight.

Dmitry watched Richard for a moment and then he stated, "That table is unique, and I know quality workmanship. Did you carve this piece?" he asked with admiration in his eyes. "By the way, my name is Dmitry Ivanov, but call me Dmitry, please."

They both smiled and shook hands. "I am Richard, Nancy's soon-to-be-husband. I hand carve wooden pieces of almost any size and shape that either I want to make for myself or a unique piece for a customer. No two pieces are the same. This table will not fit in our marital-to-be-home."

"Oh. You have a home you are selling?" Dmitry asked with a curious look on his face. "I'm looking for a second home in the Evergreen area."

"As a matter of fact, I do have a home here in Evergreen on the northern side near Genessee. It is listed with my realtor now. Here is her business card." Richard handed Dmitry the card.

Out of sheer curiosity, Richard asked Dmitry about the type of home and the size he was looking for.

"I would love to find a modernized log home with two levels and decking, detached two car garage with a lot of open space so that I can have the pleasure to watch the elk and other wildlife during the day and at sunset."

"I suggest you call my realtor. She will know what is available. My home for sale is partially modernized and is made of log and river stone. I do not have full second floor, but I have an exceptionally large loft, and open space on the west and north sides."

"Thank you, Richard. I will give her a call later this week."

Dmitry finally settled on a large (60" x 30") and lovely waterfall and mountain landscape setting done in oil, framed perfectly in a barnwood custom frame, for $12,000 K. "This is beautiful, and it will look perfect in my dining room in Denver."

Nancy rang up the purchase as Kim wrapped the painting in heavy brown paper and packing tape.

"Here you are, Dmitry, and thank you. I will hold the door open, Richard can carry one end, and help you position it in your *Bentley*.

Please come back whenever you wish to. It was lovely to meet you." Kim smiled at Dmitry and the others agreed. Dmitry gave off a genuine smile in return.

Genuine…for sure looked genuine…harmless…a true gentleman…and he is loaded…he can buy more art whenever he wants to…heck…I will open the gallery after hours for him…Kim laughed at herself, internally…of course…humor is good for the soul…

"I am famished. It is noon. Want to turn the sign to closed and pop into Creekside Smokehouse for lunch?" Paul asked. He knew he could 'crutch' his way there and back.

"Let's go!" Richard agreed and Nancy flipped the sign before Kim locked the gallery door.

They were shown to a private booth with a view of the lake from inside Creekside Smokehouse, a fine dining establishment. They offered seafood, steak, BBQ, vegetarian, and local fresh caught trout.

"How about the BBQ Nachos of tortilla chips covered in a creamy cheese sauce over chopped brisket, topped with BBQ baked beans, cheddar cheese, tomato, smoked jalapeno, onion, and drizzled in their epic BBQ sauce for our appetizer?" Paul looked at the other three to see if they agreed.

"You know that is a huge platter! With the plates they serve for each diner, I think my meal will be just this appetizer." Kim replied, then giggled.

"What's so funny?" Paul was puzzled as he peered at Kim and Nancy in turn. "You don't want an appetizer?"

"Correct me if I'm wrong, Kim, but I think she wants you to know how much food the appetizer alone will contain, and you aren't exactly active right now Paul, so…" Nancy peered over her menu at Paul, then she cracked up with a laugh.

"Oh boy, understood. I will watch my tummy NOT grow bigger," and Paul winked at his wife who was smiling and trying not to laugh as hard as Nancy was laughing, and failing in her attempt… *Leave it to Nancy to get right to the point…*

Paul ordered the BBQ Cubano on a toasted hoagie roll, yellow mustard, dill pickle, smoked ham and pulled pork, Swiss cheese, and BBQ sauce.

Nancy and Richard decided to share their meal of Bourbon Glazed Salmon, a fourteen-ounce salmon filet, blackened, and served with cilantro-lime rice and special roasted corn stuffed tater tots in their signature sauce.

Nancy opted for sparkling water, the other three ordered Chardonnay, and the waiter left to get their orders placed. Lunch was leisurely and most talk was of Nancy and Richard's upcoming wedding.

Richard was elated. Dmitry had looked at his house, and he bought it outright and in cash. Closing would happen in 30 days. Dmitry also chose carved wood furniture pieces from the gallery that he loved. Dmitry was a true gentleman in word and manner. The carved furniture was marked as sold and would be delivered after the sale closed.

July 25th was coming up fast, as in one week! The bride and groom were elated and had *lovey-dovey-eyes* whenever they were together.

"Did we have *lovey-dovey-eyes* Paul?" Kim laughed, and her husband heartily joined in and laughed.

"If you recall, we had a fast surprise engagement proposal, that you and I only knew was going to happen, and our wedding at Christmas.

We barely had time to arrange that!" Paul smiled at the memory of that evening after a huge grand opening and gallery art show.

Kim remembered their special night…the Leawood's and their family had been a big help with the grand opening/gallery showing last December 23, and when the gallery closed, only the Leawood's with Danny, Lisa, Alice, and Sadie remained inside besides Nancy and Richard, and an older man over in the southeast corner… that was curious when the gallery door was then locked…

Paul had gotten down on one knee and proposed to Kim, she accepted and after Kim said "yes", the minister (the older man) broke in with "Dearly Beloved…" Shortest engagement ever! Less than one minute! Less than 30 seconds!

Because of the gallery showing, everyone was already dressed to the nines! After the wedding, horse led sleighs took everyone around the Heart of Evergreen Lake before families headed home.

Richard had arranged the carved wood pieces that he and Nancy chose to keep, in places Nancy thought looked best, inside their marital-to-be-home. She had a keen eye for that kind of detail and Richard had no problem with where the pieces were placed.

Director James Tilson, of Homeland Security, had made a point of speaking with everyone that he had detained, for safety, in an FBI bunker at Denver Federal Center, at least once every two weeks, and he dined on occasion at their different homes. They were his family, his only family.

The adults were on a first name basis and the children called him 'Uncle James'. They were all part of the same family, and family is not always blood, as proved by this group of special people.

Those who love you and you love back, those who you want to keep intricately connected with and they wanted the same with you, those who made the effort for a familial relationship for each other, or had a special bond with, were family. This group met all those qualifiers and quite a few more.

And James would have the honor of walking Nancy down the aisle to meet her groom and soulmate. She was like a daughter to James, one he had never had as the military had been his life, and he never had a chance to fall in love or marry. He hoped he did not have wet eyes when she married. That would not look right for the Director of Homeland Security at the Denver Federal Center.

Chapter Ten

It was the 25th of July and things were well under way at the Lake House. Kim, Sarah, Alice, and Sadie did the decorating, and one staff person, Greg, provided oversight for the wedding.

All Lake House events had a staff person watching over everything as the Lake House was special, made of Montana lodgepole pine, and no nails, screws, or tape/adhesive were allowed.

The rental fee was the largest expense, at $8000 K, but all the tables, chairs, ceremony area, and Wi-Fi were included along with the staff member, Greg, who oversaw this event.

The Evergreen Lake House was decked out with battery operated fairy lights, and battery-operated candles of different sizes were placed on the tables covered in light blue linens.

The setting was perfect for the charm of a mountain wedding with evening and night lake reflections – Nancy's dream wedding and Richard was happy with anything Nancy wanted.

The great room, which seats 200 people maximum, had only 20 people for the bride and grooms' special moment. Plenty of space for dancing and the large stone fireplace served to keep the cooler lake chills away. Even in late July, lake breezes can be chilly now and then.

A buffet meal was set up in the smaller octagon room that overlooked the fantastic alpine lake that had become home. Alice and Sadie made the food items at the Leawood home and transported them to the venue as no cooking was allowed inside the venue.

The finger buffet included a variety of cold-cut small finger sandwiches of including roast beef, ham, and turkey, with a variety of cheeses, sauces, and toppings.

The canapés included caviar or choice of cheese, and the vol-au-vents were flaky and decadent - the true retro hors d'oeuvres of the season (no wedding cake), as Nancy and Richard truly made their wedding their own.

Nancy insisted on sparkling water over alcoholic beverages, especially because of the winding canyon road they would drive back home on, and plenty of hot cocoa for the children, especially.

The deck was trimmed with battery operated fairy lights around the log railings, and battery-operated candles on each flagstone step to the grassy area below.

Nancy hired a harpist to play before, during, and after the ceremony.

In true Nancy style, she opted to wear a *Vera Wang* vintage champagne short lace wedding dress with lace sleeves of a light maple color. The full skirt was knee length and showed off her shapely legs.

Nancy completed this part of her look with champagne heels from *Ralph Lauren*. The supple leather of the round toe, spool style 3-1/2" high heel, with ankle straps gave secure footing for dancing. An elegant *Vera Wang Bridal Cap* Headpiece with birdcage veil – in champagne of course sat atop her pixie cut black hair.

The final touches for something borrowed, and old, she wore an antique cameo set in yellow gold around her neck, that Alice wore when she got married oh-so-many-years-ago.

Not to be outdone, Sadie insisted that Nancy carry her blue lace edged handkerchief tucked into her bridal bouquet of champagne roses.

Kim rounded things out with a sexy champagne colored lace garter for Richard to find later that night. *The look was pure Nancy…soon she would marry Mr. Tall, Dark, and Handsome…*

As for the groom, Richard wore a three-piece blue *Armani* suit with a white shirt and blue tie. His only adornment was a champagne-colored rose boutonniere that matched his champagne-colored boots. *Men are so much easier to dress for weddings…*

No one else wore flowers and no one was allowed to throw confetti, rose petals, and the like, as the Lake House did not allow this. *Rules are rules…and this was simpler and easier for all, especially Danny and Lisa…*

Kim wore an off-the-shoulder knee length flowy dress made of emerald silk that matched her emerald-colored leather stilettos. Her blonde hair was up in a chignon with ringlets, and she wore the matching emerald and diamond necklace and bracelet set that Paul had gifted her last Valentine's Day. *Always on her ring finger was the beautiful marquise cut diamond wedding rings from Paul…*

Nine-year-old Lisa matched Kim in dress and shoe color and her shoes had a ½ inch block heel for sturdiness. *Lisa felt like a princess…*

Danny sported a new dark blue blazer with a white shirt and dark blue pants and brown boots. *No tie…just the minimum for him…Danny was happy to wear the minimum…he wanted to get the show started…the adults were taking too long…ugh…boring…*

Paul, who had just had his cast removed the day before (for being on good behavior and healing fast), now used a carved cane for added support as his leg continued to mend. His Armani suit was emerald in color to match his wife. *Oh, how sweet is that? Too sugary? Maybe…maybe not…many couples liked to pair colors at events…*

Aaron chose a dark blue suit and tie, tasteful yet casual. Sarah had slipped on a lovely V neck midi dress in a floral chiffon and wedges that matched her dress and was perfect for this casual wedding. Pearls adorned her neck and ears.

Alice wore a light pink floor length dress made of chiffon with matching flats, and Sadie decided on a bright yellow chiffon gown and yellow flats. Both wore earrings and necklaces that matched their soft, flowy, and cozy gowns.

Uncle James arrived with perfect timing dressed in a dark blue suit with a white shirt, and light blue tie. He wore a huge grin when he saw Nancy!

Chapter Eleven

It was time! The harpist started playing soft music as the guests made their way to their seats for the wedding.

Each seat had a personalized wedding favor created by Nancy and Richard waiting for them. Nancy had handmade paper cut white doves floating inside hand carved walnut frames created by Richard, with a clear plastic covering protecting the doves from damage. *Beautiful…ornate…cheesy…and unique…*

Uncle James escorted Nancy down the short aisle to her groom. Kim was already waiting next to the preacher as she was matron of honor.

Everyone smiled. Uncle James might have had the biggest smile of them all as he gave Nancy's hand to Richard standing next to his best man, Dr. Paul.

The preacher, Earl Snow, started the ceremony and traditional vows were used. "May I present Mr. and Mrs. Richard Manse. You may kiss the bride."

Richard gave Nancy a sweet and tender kiss before telling her he had some naughty ideas floating around inside his head, which caused Nancy to blush.

Then Kim said she had overheard what Richard had said, and Dr. Paul said he did, too. Nancy had beet red cheeks when the preacher informed the group that he had overheard it too! Hard laughing commenced.

That started a laughing frenzy among all in attendance and the children wanted to know what was so funny. Alice said she would find out and tell them when the time was right, and that the wedding was still in process.

Nancy and Richard walked back up the short isle arm in arm and then they gathered near a lovely wooden arch with white fairy lights wrapped around it.

"All single people must stand in front of Nancy." Richard looked around and no one got up. He decided to call them by name as Nancy wanted to toss her bouquet.

"I need Alice, Sadie, Danny, Lisa, and Uncle James front and center now!" Richard laughed as they all walked up and took their designated place.

Nancy turned around and tossed her bouquet over the top of her head, then turned around to see who had caught it. Alice caught it! She wore a shocked expression on her face, but she acted like it was no big deal.

Uncle James gave Alice a wink that was seen by Nancy and Richard only.

What was that about? Something going on that I have missed seeing...maybe... or not...hm...time will tell...sooner rather than later...

The harpist resumed playing and everyone chose what they wanted from the cold finger food buffet. Danny managed his plate perfectly, Lisa needed a little help, as did Dr. Paul with his cane.

Uncle James gave the first toast to the happy couple, and he was near tears of happiness. Happiness was overdue.

This was perfect...after the assassin tried to take them out...staying the night in a bunker at the Denver Federal Center...his job and duty as the Director of Homeland Security at the center...it was the perfect time for the group to be happy...

Kim's smart phone beeped so she took a quick glance at it and saw that the security alarm system at her gallery was going off.

Puzzled, she glanced at Paul and showed him her phone. "Call the police, Kim. It could be nothing but call them to come and check it out."

Before Kim could place the call, her mobile phone rang.

"Turn your phone off, Kim! This is our wedding!" Nancy told Kim with mock horror on her face. Then she laughed.

I have a ginormous surprise announcement to make, so she had better get off the phone fast…on the double! Richard does not even know this little tidbit…yes…a tiny tidbit…a very tiny tidbit…a peanut if you will…

"I'll take it outside." Kim stepped out the deck door and answered her phone.

It was the Chief of Police, David Spears. "Mrs. Smith, your security alarm is going off at the gallery. Officers are headed there now."

"Thank you, Chief Spears. It is just an animal – a bear. I am at the Lake House right now, so I am close by, if needed."

"I will call you back when we know anything. Please do not go to the gallery now. Stay safe. I will call you back." Chief Spears made it clear that a person or a bear was NOT the right person or animal Kim should mess with right now.

"The security alarm is going off at the gallery. Officers are checking it out now. A bear tried to get in." Kim whispered to Paul.

James overheard Kim's whisper and asked if she wanted him to check it out as well. The gallery was less than three blocks away.

"No, James. We are here as family, for Nancy and Richard's big moment, and the officers will let me know what they find out. I am sure it was a bear that set it off. No food items were left out and the trash is binned outside in the bearproof bins at close of business each day. You know how sensitive electronic security systems can be." Kim smiled at James.

Paul agreed with his wife. If a bear broke a window or did damage, the police would tell them, and then temporary metal bars and lumber would be installed to get them through the night until repairs were made the next day.

Aaron and James would have to put the temporary repair in place, if needed… he knew with his cane…never mind he'd not been cleared for work and doing his job as a neurosurgeon…not yet…unfortunately, it wasn't going to be him…not Paul to rescue his wife's gallery…that irked him just a little bit…

Chief Spears arrived at the Lake House to talk with Kim and Paul. "Can we talk outside?"

"Sure, Paul and I can chat outside. It was a bear, right?" Kim questioned.

"Not quite. We need to talk privately." Chief Spears was insistent.

"I'll go with you," James added as he sensed something more complex had happened. He had had a bad feeling for a couple of months now and he had not been unable to nail that feeling down.

Ever since the assassin, Jeffrey Sanders, or whatever his real name was, tried to kill Dr. Paul, on Memorial Day Weekend, he had poured over all the intel he had, which included the killing of persons in Boston. He tried to see what he had missed but all the t's were crossed and the i's dotted. *Still…his gut told him otherwise…and that worried him…*

"Keep on dancing and eating everyone, we need to discuss the mess the hungry bear created when it looked for food. Back shortly." Kim smiled at everyone with a chuckle.

"A hungry bear is NOT apropos for my wedding, Kim! I also will not be around to clean up a bear patty at the gallery!" Nancy laughed, as she knew that Richard and she would be headed to Paris for the start of their two-week European honeymoon.

Nancy was positive that no bears were invited…no bear patty piles for her to clean up…lots of loving and living going on…yes, the sex would be just as, if not, better…especially if Richard keeps on looking at me like I'm naked…men…the only thing on their mind…now THAT would be apropos on their honeymoon…

Richard knew his new wife and her mind was in the gutter…oh Nancy, and you force mine to go right in that gutter with you…when we get home…watch out…this groom is waiting and ready…Richard knew that he was a bit aroused…maybe they should check out of here fast…make our getaway…start our honeymoon…

Once outside, Chief Spears informed the three of them that it was not a bear or any animal.

"Someone attempted to interfere with your high-tech security system. In other words, they tried to jam the frequency, and without success as they made their way inside. I am so sorry this happened. The person (s) got away right before we arrived." The chief sighed.

"Upon checking out the premises inside and out, we found one damaged piece of art, and it does not make any sense. The perpetrator stole a wooden frame off one painting and took it with him, leaving the painting behind which is odd as paintings are more costly and worth much more than a frame." Chief Spears was puzzled.

From that discourse, James knew something big might be in the works and that the FBI and Homeland Security would come with one phone call from him. Not what one wants to find out during a wedding reception. James went into director mode.

"Kim, I have had a feeling since the day I met you at the Denver Federal Center, that more might happen. We need to have a safe discussion now with everyone present." After grabbing his mobile phone from his pocket, he continued, "I am calling for Homeland Security to come here ASAP to assess the crime scene and to protect the Lake House occupants from being hurt or worse. Everyone must go back inside, now."

"Excuse me?" Chief Spears was confused. "Who are you and what are you talking about? I do not take orders from you!"

"I am Director James Tilson of Homeland Security at The Denver Federal Center. Once inside, I will explain. As of now, and possibly temporarily, I have taken over the Lake House and all occupants. Homeland Security will assume duties at the gallery when they arrive via helicopter and armored SUVs with the FBI doing the collection of intelligence and evidence." Director Tilson hustled everyone on the deck indoors quickly.

Kim's heart went into fast mode…not again…not a third time…no way…nope…not going to happen…but what if James is right…what value is a wooden frame taken off a painting…it makes no sense…leave the painting untouched…take the frame with you…

Chapter Twelve

Once inside the Lake House, Director Tilson got the group's attention with his booming voice. The preacher had left earlier so he was safe. "Please have a seat everyone and that includes the harpist and, Greg, you need sit with them as well. Before you sit, please turn off all the lights so that only the candles and fairy lights are on."

Bewildered, Greg did as he was told and then sat down with the rest of the wedding party. *What is going on….*

Nancy was horrified and the shock showed on her face. *Why now… why again…this is too much…I do not believe it…things were going so well…not at my wedding of all places…no…*

Richard was confused and did his best to console his new wife. *I thought this mess was done and over with…please, Lord, let us all be safe…*

Aaron, Sarah, and the children, Danny, and Lisa, sat together with Alice and Sadie next to them. They wore mute expressions and waited for the director to speak.

Kim and Paul sat near Director Tilson and Chief Spears.

Director Tilson asked everyone to remain calm. Then he informed them that someone attempted to interfere with the high-tech security system at the gallery. They had tried to jam the frequency, without success, as they made their way inside.

"I am so sorry this happened. The person(s) got away right before we arrived." Chief Spears sighed.

With a nod of yes from Director Tilson, the chief continued, "We checked inside and outside the gallery. One window was broken, out of irritation that their jamming device had failed. Other than that, we found one damaged piece of art, and it does not make any sense." He shook his head before he continued.

"I am puzzled. The burglar removed a wooden frame off one painting and took it with him, leaving the painting behind. The painting was more costly than the frame they took."

"That is where I stepped in. Chief Spears is right. Why take a frame and leave the painting behind? It makes no sense at all. My men will assess and then the next step will be decided. I do not want the lights on for now, because the break-in is more suspicious of someone wanting to find a certain item, not as a burglar's MO would normally be."

Director Tilson added, "This could be over in less than one hour. Out of caution, please stay seated and discuss this among each other. Grab some food from the finger buffet and sit back down. No music, though, as I want to be able to hear what is going on outside, if anything should go on, and I do not suspect that will be an issue. Yet we are sitting ducks here in the Lake House. Chief Spears has this house and area secured with extra men. We are all safe for now. And the chief and I want to keep everyone safe. Understood?" All heads present nodded in agreement as they watched the director and his face.

"Kim, I have studied all the facts and files on the case involving the hits ordered on those in Boston and the two attempts on Paul's life here in Colorado. I question myself on what key piece I might have missed if there is one."

"I remember reading about that case, Director," replied Chief Spears. "I don't see a connection, but I also don't have the training the FBI or Homeland Security has."

This doesn't make sense…what did I miss…the reasoning, in an assassin's mind, of taking out Kim was understandable…especially if Steve and Gary thought Kim knew about plans on the president…the deranged reasoning in the handler's mind was understandable in a psychotic sense…am I looking at this too deep? Now was the time to keep everyone safe… again…

Director Tilson's phone beeped, and he stepped away from the table as he answered. After speaking with the agents, he hung up and went back to the table.

"The only thing taken was the frame that held a seascape. Per the FBI, one wooden frame was removed from a painting, and the painting was left behind at the scene."

"What painting," Kim asked. "Each piece has the artist's name and details on a card next to it."

"It was a smaller but beautiful scenic landscape piece left to lay on the top of the cash register, the card had the name of 'Emma Pleasance', and it was noted as not for sale. The cash register had not been messed with. The painting had zero damage, as if the perpetrator cared about the value and creativity of the art itself."

"That was one of my mom's newer pieces, painted a few weeks before she died in a car crash with my dad, Donald. Do you remember I mentioned they died in a suspicious crash? The'd just arrived back in Boston for my wedding to Steve, only a couple of weeks before my wedding, and after coming home from a successful three-week art showing in London. Her works were displayed, and mom and dad were on hand at the gallery in London each day."

What now…have not we had enough…this is nuts…why would anyone want a wood frame…Geesh…people can be so stupid…

"Hm, that is true. You did say something about that. Please explain what happened again." The Director wanted to know the facts as Kim knew them to be.

"Well, their car went over the side of a ravine, and both died on impact. No skid marks, no black ice, dry roadway, no rain or fog, the temperature had been in the upper 40s, and nothing was in the roadway to indicate my dad had anything to do with the crash, no dead animals, nothing. He was a careful driver. They died only one week after my wedding. It was late September, and it was not even dark out. They died on impact, and…" Kim wiped at the tears that streamed down both of her cheeks.

"Take your time, Kim. I know this is terribly traumatic for you to relive. Was their home broken into?" Director Tilson was doing his best to figure out a connection, if any, existed, and he tried to make his questions the least traumatic he could, if that were even possible.

"We came back from our honeymoon early after being notified of the crash and subsequent deaths. I was in their house a few days after they died; they had left everything to me as an only child." Kim wiped away more tears and thought she had raccoon eyes by now. *Not the time to try and joke around…her parents were the apples of her eyes…she missed them so much…she loved them dearly…*

"Easy, Kim. Do not leave anything out. I intend to do my own investigation on the crash as well as the paintings issue and obtain information from those involved." Director Tilson replied. He wanted to console her the best he could, but he was in director mode, so Paul had that job on him alone, to help his wife. Nancy held Kim's left hand tightly.

"The strangest thing I noted was that mom's paintings were stacked on top of each other oddly and not how paintings should be stored or placed for storage; they were not in a dark protected room with art storage racks to separate each piece. I mean, they would have been wrapped and taped for the trip back from London, and then stored in a climate-controlled room they had for her artworks, in storage racks made for paintings to be stored."

Kim took a deep breath. "It made no sense to see them stacked on top of each other, but I could not exactly ask my mom or dad about it. I thought it strange that some of mom's paintings did not have frames on them, let alone not wrapped up. Paper and tape were strewn about the room. That was not mom or dad's style." She glanced at the director, and he encouraged Kim to keep telling her story.

Someone did that on purpose during a search…looking for something…and I just now realize why the mess was a mess…it had to be the same person(s) who did that to my parent's house…the same one(s) my art gallery…must be connected…but how and why? This is odd…

"All of mom's works were framed for the London gallery showing and they only brought back unsold framed pieces, wrapped in brown paper, and taped. Do you think someone was looking for something in the frames that were taken? What would be of such great value and how would it even be hidden in a frame, whatever that 'it' was?"

Could mom's art have anything to do with the crash…this mess has ruined Nancy's wedding…another disaster…out of her control…and all her fault…more tears slid down Kim's cheeks and Paul gently blotted them with a tissue…

"It was the same person at my parent's house and my gallery. You see the connection, don't you?" Kim demanded an answer.

"This investigation has just started. It is too early to know of any connections. I will research this myself, and let you know what I find out." The director's phone rang again, and he answered, while still seated at the table. After a few 'yes' answers and a 'no', plus one 'I see' response, he hung up.

"Your mom's painting was not damaged, Kim, and my men could only ascertain that the frame itself was taken, nothing else in the gallery. Considering these facts, your parents' manner of dying, her paintings disordered, not stored properly, some with missing frames, and after a three-week London art showing, they 'could be' connected. I will contact Scotland Yard about this. The perpetrator was not after any of you. Thanks to You, Jesus." Director Tilson smiled at everyone.

"Go ahead and turn the lights back on, Greg. We should close this party now. Sorry Nancy and Richard. I am having each family escorted back home. You will drive your own vehicles, with an FBI or Homeland Security escort, home tonight, and go about your business as usual in the morning. They will only escort you home and then leave."

'Yay!" Danny and Lisa yelled in unison. They were both tired and ready for things to be over with.

"Well, I guess Richard and I don't have to sneak away now to start our honeymoon." Nancy snickered. "We'll be escorted home and tomorrow we fly to Paris!" Everyone laughed!

"You said it, Babe," and Richard gave Nancy a sassy wink and grin. *Honeymoon time…such a delectable delight…*

"Get a room already!" Kim replied before she cracked up laughing and the others joined in laughing with amusement.

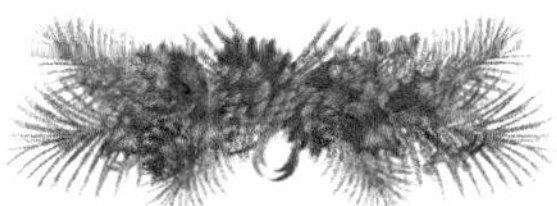

The Lake House was cleaned well as is the norm for renting it, and everyone went home, the only difference was having an FBI escort. The FBI secured the broken window, and Director Tilson turned the situation back over to the Evergreen Chief of Police.

Chapter Thirteen

*N*ancy slowly woke up two days later in their hotel room at The Ritz Paris. Richard was placing soft kisses on her cheeks, eye lids, and lips. "Again, Richard?"

"Well, we have no exact timetable to do or see the city so, when in the City of Love, one should make love often, right?"

"Touché," she smiled back at Richard. "Beat you to the shower!"

And off she ran full of giggles, with Richard on her tail.

"Soapy sex in the shower and such spontaneity is perfect." Richard started soaping up Nancy with sensual touches. One thing led to another, and they had made love twice more before getting out of their sumptuous bed.

They had a spacious and luxurious room, but not one of the named rooms or suites. The luxury hotel was framed in fine gold leaf and delicately embroidered florals. The satin-soft Italian sheets and bedding was completely sumptuous, and perfect to sleep in, wake up in, or other things normal honeymooners do.

Who would not love their room with its marble fireplace, fancy gilt mirrors everywhere, a bathroom to die for and the languorous light that peeked through the elegant, framed windows.

Thus far, they had been too busy to sit at either reading/writing nooks, but they did view the beautiful paintings that adorned the walls of their beautiful room.

When they finally came up for air, they decided that The Butte Montmartre was the place to go first. Loved-up couples enjoyed the view of the city's rooftops from the foot of the Sacré-Cœur Basilica, as much as they did when they had arrived two hours earlier.

"Yum…we chose the perfect city and the perfect spot for today. I love you." Nancy murmured to Richard when their lips parted after a sensual kiss.

"I love you more, Nancy. Everything feels right. No worries. Just us." Richard winked in a sexy way at Nancy.

Nancy snickered, "I thought you were more perceptive than that. Haven't you learned anything over the last three months? Have you never even suspected one single thing?" Then she laughed, more giggles spilled over as his expression kept changing.

Nancy had originally planned to tell him her suspicions back at the end of May, but The Federal Center happened…then she decided to blow Richard's and everyone's minds right after their wedding…but then the gallery was broken into… so now it will be…

"Okay, I give up. What did I miss?" Richard was perplexed. Nancy had a way of puzzling him in a fun manner any chance she got. That was one of the many things he loved about her. "Well? Are you going to clue me in or not, woman?"

"We have spent the last three months having a lot of sex, especially the last nine weeks together every night, even before Memorial Day. Each of those nights we made love and I fell asleep in your arms." Nancy looked Richard in the eyes, and she hoped he would figure it out, sooner rather than later. *Bingo! Talk about ginormous eyes! Could they get any bigger?*

"Nancy! You have not had a period! Are you pregnant?" The look of shock on Richard's face was priceless. Priceless, precious, and perfect. *Oh yes…he got it…*

"Yes!!! I wanted to tell you about my suspicions at the end of May, but then the assassin caused problems and we stayed at the Denver Federal Center. I took a home pregnancy test and it was positive. I was afraid that the stress of what we went through would cause me to lose our baby, so I went to my new obstetrician, Dr. Tammy Harwell, and she said I am okay."

After she took in a deep breath of air, Nancy continued, "Then we were full on in planning our wedding, and I was praying my wedding dress would still fit me, plus I wasn't having any morning sickness, and I decided to tell you late in the evening on our wedding day, as a special wedding gift to you from me, but then things happened at the Lake House…"

Nancy had to take another deep breath as she ran out of steam. The time to tell Richard was never quite right. They were both busy little bees getting things in order before their big day. Moving and arranging Richard's carved art into their home had to be done and the gallery was busy.

Nancy was worried as Richard did not say anything. "Are you okay? Are you okay with us having a baby? Do you even want a baby?" Richard had to say yes. He had to as Nancy had wanted a baby for a couple of years already. *He just had to say yes…if he could not manage it, she would do it on her own…*

"Oh yes, I am indeed. Until I met you, I thought I would never marry or be a father!" Richard gave Nancy a tender kiss and placed his hands upon her stomach, her tummy that had been flat, and now sported a tiny baby bump.

"Wow, how did I not notice this little baby bump? We have been having a lot of sex. Will that hurt the baby?" Richard was worried.

"My doctor said sex was fine, unless I start spotting or something, and if we don't have some weird kinky kind of sex." She grinned up at Richard, then broke out laughing, and caused Richard to laugh with her.

"Okay. Weird and kinky is out for now." Richard swept Nancy into his arms for a ginormous hug. *Life was wonderful…and it kept on getting better and better…my woman…carrying my baby…*

"Richard! Have you NOT noticed my breasts are a bit fuller? A bit more tender? My face glows – did you really miss that?" she smiled at her husband as she gently cupped his face in her delicate hands. *This is the most special moment in my life, ever…*

"That comes with being pregnant, right? Yes? No? You have that 'pregnancy glow' I heard about. I thought it was because we were getting married. Plainly the baby causes the glow and not me. I am hurt." Richard smiled down at Nancy. "Actually, you have the glow of pregnancy AND of a new bride AND of the wonderful and splendiferous sex this morning, all sudsy and soapy."

After another wink at his wife, he replied. "I must thoroughly check your breasts out when we get back to our room. Yes. Thoroughly. I must know what our baby will be in for." Richard huskily spoke into Nancy's ears.

"Well? Don't you have more to tell me? The doctor had to give you a due date. When? I want to start carving our baby's new crib as soon as we get back." *I do not care if it is a boy or a girl... Nancy is giving me the best gift...I love my woman...my Nancy...my baby...*

"Evidently, I got pregnant around April 1st – no joke. And... I am due on Christmas Day – no joke!" She squinted her eyes at Richard who sported the biggest grin ever. Did Richard believe her about April Fool's Day and Christmas?

He kissed Nancy on the lips, soft, tender, and sensual, not sloppy and all tongue. A tender kiss for his love. "A Christmas baby; life is so good for us." Richard held his wife tight, and they finished the day talking about their hopes and dreams, and all things baby-ish before they sat down at their table, in the hotel's Espadon Restaurant.

They dined on exquisite delicacies that started with appetizer of radish-peanut-and green cardamom combo with a sunny fragrance. Then the oyster-Brede Mafane-Brousse Cheese fresh off the grill and Lobster-Casava-Bissap BBQed on the grill with a special acidulated manioc seed bisque and hibiscus flower.

They toasted with sparkling water and had a delicious and iconic vanilla caramel Ritz au lait – a truly exquisite combination of all things vanilla, almond, caramel, and white chocolate.

Chapter Fourteen

While Nancy and Richard wrapped up their Parisian honeymoon, the house in Evergreen closed, and Dmitry took possession.

In true Dmitry style, he had all the wood pieces carved by Richard, and bought at Kim's gallery, delivered to his new home. He also bought two more paintings, one created by Kim and the other from an area artist, for his new home.

Everything was in place. Now he had to wait and continue to play the part of a super kind and super rich Russian for many months.

If they only knew…yet they were clueless…apparently, he was not on their radar at all…the way he preferred to fly…when undercover…and he was determined to find the right frames…only two frames carried the intel…если бы они только знали…if only they knew…

Dmitry took advantage of buying new art pieces every month from Kim's gallery. On each visit, he would look at the paintings on the walls created by Kim's mother as well, particularly their frames, albeit in a surreptitious manner. He remained congenial and no one thought anything of him, as he had become a friend.

The entire group had placed Dmitry into the category of "nice-human-super-rich-Russian-gentleman-who-loved-Evergreen-and-appreciated/collected-art. Chatting with Dmitry and sipping coffee or tea at the gallery was normal for all. *они были невежественны…they were ignorant, indeed…*

Director James had even met Dmitry at the gallery early in August. Uncle James thought Dmitry was an exemplary, kind, and sociable

Russian gentleman. He presented himself as considerate, rich, caring, with absolutely nothing suspicious about him.

Yet, James took it upon himself to investigate Dmitry's background. He wanted no stones left unturned. After deep digging between the FBI, CIA, and Homeland Security, Dmitry proved himself to be exactly what he appeared to be. *I will keep my eye on him whenever I see him…just to make sure… no one needs to know my special little spy-op, the director thought…no harm, no foul…*

Little did they know…if only London had worked out…it will take many months, but it will work out as planned…after all, Dmitry was living in the area that held the frames he needed…and money was of no concern…no concern at all… the Russian oligarch that he was…

Paul went back to work. His leg had healed enough for him to do so, and he no longer required a cane to get around. He had missed the ER for way too long. Paul was careful, but then Sarah would ride his butt if she thought he was overdoing it.

That is the price you pay when your best friend, Aaron, an ER doctor, was married to Sarah, an ER nurse. Of course, he only saw them when neuro related traumas arrived in the ER bay or when the four of them got together for a meal and drinks.

Sarah was back working her shifts as an RN in the ER. August was a hectic month. School supplies, and new clothes for school were needed since school would start in only two weeks!

Alice was a huge help in sorting out what the children needed, and Sadie washed and organized the supplies with help from both kids. Together they filled boxes with clothes Danny and Lisa had outgrown, and donated them to Catholic Charities, a favorite one that Sarah donated to regularly.

The Saturday before the start of school, Nancy, Richard, and Uncle James were with the Leawood family for dinner that evening. He had been seeing all three couples regularly since Nancy and Richard's wedding.

Richard looked forward to each time he was with them, mostly due to how he considered them each part of his own family, but he also enjoyed having lively discussions with Alice, a keen reader of all books.

That evening they enjoyed a delicious meal of tender pork chops with a creamy parmesan sauce, buttered new potatoes, green beans sautéed with sliced cherry tomatoes, rolls, and praline ice cream for dessert.

James loved the ambiance of their dining room with exposed beams in the vaulted ceiling, and the rich color of their large rectangular pecan dining table that seated twelve people with ease. The gleam of the table was evident in the light of the various sized candles and the soft lighting of a chandelier above the table.

James loved to see the family pictures on the walls of the great room as they leant a coziness known by a family who loved each other very much.

Tinkling heard with a fork on a glass that Richard held, got the attention of everyone. "Nancy and I have an announcement." Smiling at his bride of over one month, he motioned for Nancy to finish their announcement.

"We're preggers!!!" Nancy squealed with joy. "I have a little baby bump and a baby bean growing inside of me," and she showed off her bump to those present around the table.

Congratulations went on for a while and then Sarah spoke. "As a nurse, and as a mother, I knew you were pregnant, Nancy! I saw your beautiful pregnancy glow, the tiny baby bump, and your breasts a bit fuller." Then she giggled. "Took you long enough to tell us!"

Kim snickered and added, "Yeah, we all saw the signs, but we waited for you to spill the beans, your tiny little baby bean, in your own time. Tell us the rest already, will you? We all know you are still hiding a bean here and there! Not your baby bean growing."

"Our baby is due on Christmas Day!" Nancy and Richard smiled at everyone with blissful happiness.

"How utterly divine and wonderful," exclaimed Alice. "A new baby at Christmas time. Perfect."

"A new baby due on the First Day of Christmas." Sadie smiled and clapped her hands a couple of times.

"Will the baby be my cousin, Aunt Nancy?" Lisa's blue eyes were more than ginormous as she looked expectantly at Nancy, while she waited to know if Danny and she were to have a new cousin – their very first cousin!

Nancy looked at Sarah, and Sarah nodded her head in agreement. Again, both kids were told that family is not always blood. Nancy made sure that they understood that family are those people you love and want to include in your family. For all of us here right now, we are ALL family. So, yes, you will have a new cousin in about four months or so. Nancy beamed a bright grin at the happy-for-a-new-cousin-look both children gave her.

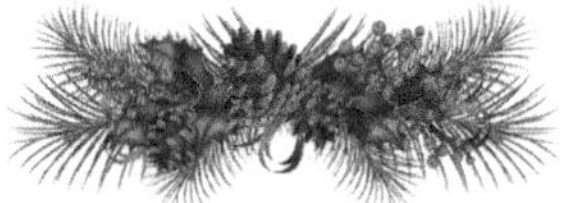

After dinner, James and Alice went over to the breakfast nook that overlooked a small lake and the two smaller log homes that belonged to Alice and Sadie, respectively.

They sat down with their glass of Pinot and watched the wildlife through the bay windows. Soft rose-colored cushions created a perfect place to read, daydream, have coffee, or even breakfast, as it was so cozy for a nook, yet open to the large dining room.

"I really like spending time with you, Alice." James wanted Alice to know he thought she was special. "We have great discussions on books you read, and chatting about the family and how things are going. You have become special to me."

What will she think…will she stop me in my tracks…this is new territory for me…I've been out of the dating game for two decades, I mean I dated, but nothing serious, sometimes a one-night stand…nothing of a need to be near a person…the wanting I feel for being near Alice…

"I enjoy the moments we share, both with family and alone, and I love it when we talk about our lives, family, and your work – the bits you can tell me. I love our deepening friendship." Alice smiled up at James' face. Does he want more?

Do I want more…it has been such a long time for me since my husband died…my nerves are on edge…a lot has been happening…but my heart says it is finally time…

"I do not know how you feel, but I want to continue our relationship as it is now and see where it leads us. I am not pressuring you at all, Alice. I simply want to savor the moments when I get them." James peered into Alice's dark eyes, trying to read her feelings.

"That sounds fine with me. I want to see where this goes naturally and not push things forward." Alice gently held James' hand, "Is that enough for you? That is all I can give you right now." *I hope he says yes…I am like a student and wanting a boy to like her…but not sure of what to do…*

"Perfect, Alice. This will give us time to see what we want out of life, and in our retirement years, whether it works out or not. I am planning on it working out simply fine," he smiled and gave Alice a tender kiss on her forehead. *That was just how he had wanted things to go…slow, easy, but moving forward…*

"Uncle James kissed Grandma!" Lisa yelled, and the entire house knew what she saw. At age nine, she was just as precocious as when younger. Everyone laughed, and Alice blushed just a bit. Sadie simply smiled a secret knowing smile, as if she had known this was coming all along, which she did know.

"Lisa! Do not watch people to see what they are doing. Leave Grandma and Uncle James alone." Aaron admonished his daughter with a smile.

All too soon, the evening ended. Alice and Sadie both went home to their cabins behind the main house, and Uncle James left for his

Lakewood home on Green Mountain. The kids had their baths and bedtime was right on track. Sarah and Aaron snuggled on the sofa for a while before going to bed. The perfect family evening and life was wonderful.

Or so they all thought…each of them was about to see another wallop strike… close to home, and not expected one little bit…

Chapter Fifteen

ancy and Richard pulled up outside the art gallery in Nancy's Velvet Red Pearl-Coated Jeep Grand Cherokee Limited with all the bells and whistles. They wanted to see if Kim needed anything as they were enroute to see Nancy's obstetrician for the first sonogram.

"All is good here, Nancy. Business is slow so I have plenty of time to help Susan learn the business. We are fine, thanks for asking.

Get that sonogram." Kim kissed Nancy's cheek and gave her a big hug. "I want to know the sex of my new niece or nephew, so get it done and spill the beans when you get back." Kim gave Nancy a saucy wink and grinned.

Susan Davis turned her head and smiled at Nancy. She had spiraling curly dark red hair with eyes of deepest green on a petite frame at five feet tall. Her face glowed with a natural freshness accented with a light sprinkling of freckles, and one would not know she was age 25 as she looked five years younger.

"Wonderful! I am so glad we decided to hire you, Susan. You fit right in, plus you are an incredibly good photographer. You have a keen eye and are great with the customers." Nancy smiled back, and as she and Richard left the gallery, they noticed Dmitry was shopping for yet more items for his new home in Evergreen. *Only a rich Russian oligarch would spend money like he did…*

Yes, and only I, Dmitry, have made it possible to look over frames of Kim's mother's paintings quickly as they no longer watched him closely…he had the money, he was their friend, and he meant to keep it that way until he found what he searched for…a very tiny little thing…two of them…cleverly hidden…but of the highest importance…it was too bad that the frame he'd stolen from the gallery didn't contain what he looked for…he would bide his time for now…besides, they were all interesting people…but he wouldn't get soft on them…not for one second…

Dr. Tammy Harwell's office was located right off Bergen Parkway and Castle Drive just north of Hiwan Heritage Park, in Evergreen.

The Hiwan Heritage Park and Museum is a great place to learn about local and state history and view the architectural features in a natural Ponderosa pine setting. The main residence was hand built by Evergreen craftsman, Jock Spence, from local materials. Started in 1893, and by 1918, had twenty-five rooms. These included two octagonal towers, a chapel, formal dining room, and many bedrooms.

After checking in at the front desk, Nancy and Richard took a seat in the waiting room. Soon the nurse, Vicky Torres, dressed in scrubs with babies on them, called out for Nancy.

After escorting Nancy and Richard into the examination room, she took Nancy's vital signs and weight. Vicky was a kind woman, and her 40 years was kind on her Latino countenance as she had very few wrinkles.

"Okay, need help to get on this exam table? Oh good, you are so strong, Nancy. The doctor will lift your shirt up when she comes in shortly." Vicky smiled and out the door she went.

Dr. Harwell came in and introduced herself to Richard. "Are you ready for your sonogram? More importantly, are you ready to find out if it is a boy or a girl?"

"Yes!" Nancy and Richard replied in unison and then they all laughed.

"Okay. Not to put things off, but I want to listen to your heart and the baby's first."

Two heartbeats noted, Dr. Harwell informed Nancy that the ultrasound gel was warmed in its place in the machine.

"I'll dim the lights now and we'll get started." Lights dimmed; she placed a towel down low below Nancy's belly. "The gel is warm, water-based, and does not stain clothing. It helps transmit sound waves more precisely than without."

She squirted warm gel onto Nancy's stomach and began to move the transducer over her baby bump. "As you know, Nancy, your first ultrasound should have been done two months ago, but I know everything that has happened. I am confident things are fine." Dr. Harwell smiled at both Nancy and Richard.

"Right now, I am taking measurements of your baby's head circumference and length. Do not worry, this is the first part of the ultrasound. I am checking placement of the placenta and a few other things." Using a mouse the doctor made lines on the monitor screen and froze some angles as pictures.

"The screen images look like x-rays," Richard commented. "I do not know what I am looking at, but I see our baby's head and legs for sure. Amazing!" Richard was spellbound and Nancy simply grinned with pure joy.

Our baby…is right there…we made this little human…this little mini…I have no words…totally awestruck…off in his own world and not listening to the doctor…

"Richard? Are you okay? Or are you in dreamland?" Nancy snickered. Then laughed at her husband. "You've not heard anything Dr. Harwell has told us."

"Sorry, so sorry." Richard replied looking a tiny bit sheepishly.

"Everything looks normal," she told the parents. "Almost done, just a bit more to go. Your baby is growing and developing normally, as expected." Dr. Harwell told both parents.

"I don't see any problems with your baby or his environment in your womb, and I see no congenital conditions or issues."

"His?" Nancy asked with wide open blue eyes.

"Oops. Yes, sorry, you are having a boy." The doctor smiled at both expectant parents.

"Yes! Oh, yes! My first baby and I hope he looks like his daddy," Nancy gushed her words out fast. Richard wore a broad grin on his face.

Dr. Harwell wiped the gel off Nancy's tummy and handed them each one sonogram picture that had printed without the proud parents knowing.

"Have you had any problems about which I should know? You told me on the phone no spotting or morning sickness, but do you have anything else I should know?" She wanted to make sure things were good all around.

"My breasts are fuller, as expected, but the right one hurts more than the left. Other than that, things are normal." Nancy answered the doctor still on a ginormous high about their baby.

"Any one spot on your right breast? Can you show me, please?"

Nancy slid her shirt over her head and removed her bra. She pointed to an area near the inside of the nipple on her right breast.

"Okay, I am going to palpate this area. I will do the left breast first, then the right." As the doctor palpated, Nancy and Richard looked at the sonogram pictures and were in total awe of the tiny human they had created.

"Ow! That hurts!" Nancy said and the doctor asked her if she had hurt her breast or ran into anything lately. No bruise was noted, but she needed facts. She had palpated a mass in the right breast, most likely ductal (milk duct) area.

"No, I have not. What are you not telling me?" At only twenty-seven, she was fearful of the worst. *Please no cancer…let this be pregnancy related…please dear Lord Jesus…please…please…I beg You…*

"I do not know what is going on. But you will have a mammogram before you leave today. Wait in here while I get that arranged." Then she was out the door and Richard held Nancy's trembling hand.

Really? Why this now…we have a tiny human…I am his mommy…it cannot be cancer…this is not acceptable…nope, not going there…tears spilled over and down both cheeks and Richard kept wiping them away and kissing her cheeks and forehead…

A mammography tech came into her room and said that she would take her to mammography and then bring her back to the same room. Richard was to wait and remain in the room.

Once the mammogram was over, Nancy was escorted back to her room, where Richard was waiting. The tech could not tell Nancy anything about the scan, so they had to wait for a radiologist to read her scans. Techs are not allowed to tell patients what they see.

Soon, Dr. Harwell came back into the room, and she had a radiology doctor with her, Dr. Timothy Holm.

"I want to do a special ultrasound on your breast," he told Nancy. "I will have both of you escorted to that room. Please do not worry, I just want to make sure we know what we are dealing with."

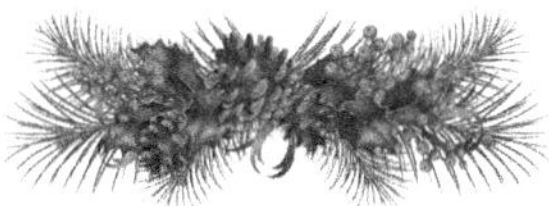

Nancy got situated on the biopsy bed and Dr. Holm positioned her breast for the best advantage to obtain films. With gel and a transducer, he moved it over the area in question, and the surrounding area, then back to the area in question again.

"It is a soft tissue swelling or mass around one of your milk ducts. That does not mean you have cancer. It does mean that you should have a thin needle biopsy done. I can do that now if you want to have it done."

Nancy was mute, tears streaming down her face as she felt that her own body had failed her unborn baby and Richard. Finally, she said yes, let us do it. Richard had to leave the room as they would set up for the sterile procedure.

Nancy was determined that no chemo or radiation would be done, as she wanted her baby boy to live...my baby will live...they can take the lump out...or cut my breast off...ASAP...

The tech set up the sterile equipment, tray, needles, and the plastic specimen container. The doctor came back in and donned a sterile gown and gloves, his mask already in place. He cleansed her nipple and the surrounding area with a surgical scrub swab in a circular motion. Then he did it again with another swab. It was important that no bacteria got into the breast from her skin.

He injected Nancy with numbing medicine, Lidocaine, around the mass area and the area in which the needle would be mechanically shot into the mass from the opposite side. Nancy did what she was told, but she stayed mute, tears running down her face.

The tech held the transducer probe out to Dr. Holm, and he placed a sterile plastic covering over the top of it, then took the probe from the tech and pulled the sterile covering the rest of the way down while the tech donned sterile gloves.

Once it was all ready, the tech held the transducer above the area of the mass and Dr. Holm took aim and obtained four specimens for biopsy.

"Tell me, tell me now, what do they look like? I want to see them." He showed Nancy the thin red strips in the specimen container.

"I am sending these off for biopsy, but I want you to know, they are red throughout and that is good. Gray areas indicate cancer or malignancy and I see none of that. It is likely that this is a simple hematoma or some other benign mass." He gave Nancy a smile as he left with the specimens in his hand.

The tech helped Nancy clean up and took her back to the room Richard waited in.

Post procedure teaching began. Using her bra to support her breast an ice pack was placed into position, and it would require replacement every 20 minutes or so, on and off, to always keep pressure on the area, and never place the ice pack directly on the skin. Use a washcloth or any soft cloth, between the ice pack and her skin.

Dr. Harwood came in and told them that it would take a few days for the biopsy results to come back. She was confident that all would be well.

Richard drove them home and it was a quiet evening. They each voiced positive thoughts to each other and held one another tenderly. Their phones were placed on mute as they wanted to be alone together. Talking with their friends right now was too much. Yet they both knew that their friends would worry about them. *Tonight, they needed each other only…it was all they could bear…*

Chapter Sixteen

Everyone was positive and upbeat for Nancy and Richard. Kim started planning a baby shower for the little, tiny human boy that would make himself known come December.

It had been easy to tell the 'family' they were having a boy, not as easy to tell them the rest. Today, the report would come back, and Dr. Harwell would call as soon as she knew anything.

Life had been on hold the last couple of days for Nancy, and she was on tenterhooks waiting to find out what they would have to deal with.

Still at home, Nancy and Richard cuddled on the sofa while waiting for Dr. Harwood's call. Nancy's phone rang and interrupted her thoughts.

"Hello," Nancy spoke softly into her mobile, waiting for the doctor's words on her mass, and with her phone in speaker mode Richard heard everything.

"Nancy, is that you?" Dr. Harwood asked.

"Yes, Dr. Harwood." Nancy replied as she looked at Richard who held her hand tightly.

"Would you please state the last four digits of your social security number and your date of birth? I must verify whom I am speaking with," Dr. Harwood continued, and Nancy spoke the numbers back.

"It is NOT cancer! You have zero signs of cancer. The mass…" Dr. Harwood stopped speaking until the shouts that Nancy and Richard gave off, stopped.

"Nancy? Are you still with me?"

"Yes, I am…we are. I have you on speaker phone. Thank you for telling us the good news."

"You are welcome. The pathologist found fat necrosis, fibrosis, and hemorrhage. He also says you are negative for atypical ductal hyperplasia, ductal carcinoma, in SITU, or invasive carcinoma. Would you like for me to explain what all of this means?" Dr. Harwood questioned Nancy.

"Yes, please and thank you." Nancy responded, still giddy with happiness over NO cancer, yet curious as to what the pathologist meant by his medical verbiage.

"Fat necrosis is an inflammation of adipose tissue (the fatty tissue of the breast) caused by the disruption of oxygen supply to fat cells. That causes cell death. How or why, it happened to you is unknown. Are you with me?" Dr. Harwood asked and both replied yes.

"Okay, you do have fibrocystic breasts which means that your breasts are starting to create small lumps that can hurt at times. You are young for this condition, but it is not unheard of in younger women. You have no need to worry about this, but I do suggest yearly mammograms as it will be more difficult to palpate an actual mass from a fibro cyst."

"I understand, Dr. Harwood." Nancy and Richard smiled at each other.

"Now, the pathologist did mention signs of a hemorrhage. That is a small collection of blood usually caused by some type of injury, breast procedure, or cosmetic breast surgery. With you, you have no recall of hurting or bumping your breast into anything. This hematoma will slowly go away on its own as the blood is reabsorbed back into your body."

"That is wonderful, Dr. Harwood. Thank you so much for explaining this to us." Richard said as Nancy kept on smiling. "But what is that 'SITU' mean?"

"In Nancy's case, SITU means no cancer was noted and/or found inside the milk duct tissue that was assessed. SITU means no cancer in one specific area."

"That makes sense, thank you for telling us. The 'medical speak' is not our areas of expertise." Richard replied, then they all had a good laugh, and mere moments later, they hung up Nancy's phone.

Overwhelmed with happiness, they phoned each household of their Colorado mountain family and gave them the great news. Everyone was elated with the joyful news. It was past time for happy news to flow around.

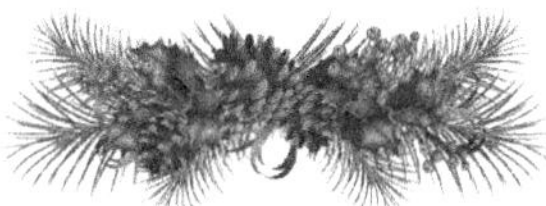

October arrived, and with it, all the lovely colors of the leaves showed themselves in the higher elevations of Colorado. With elk cows, the height of estrus occurs within several days of the Autumnal Equinox on September 21. "Estrus" causes an odorous pheromone to be released into the air that drive the bull elk crazy for a mate.

And crazy puts it mildly…trust me on this…I know how crazy they are…

Those fully antlered bulls scent this change in the air, and the rut begins. Bull elk are completely focused on mating, and they often fight each other to become king, to become the most dominant bull for all the elk in their herd. Loud Bugling is heard in RMNP and throughout Colorado.

Evergreen was no exception and the frenetic 30-day period between September 15 and October 15 is the annual Autumn Rut.

Elk hunting is easier during the rut as the males are less cautious about hunters since their focus is on the females only. All you need is a license, an area that is provided and legal for hunting, and most places are found on the western side of the divide as more elk live on that side.

It is not unusual to see two bulls with antlers down and charging as they fought for dominance. This was great for photographers, especially with the fall foliage, but one had to be careful. Give elk a wide birth as they are unpredictable at best.

Dmitry loved the magnificent and majestic elk, and he watched from the lap of luxury in his mountain home. He watched how the deer, large birds, occasional eagles, rabbits, ground squirrels, coyotes, and more go about their busy days and into the late evenings. The fireplace was cozy, the air a clean and refreshing pine scent.

Not like Russia…at all…he would miss Evergreen when he left…he would even miss the friends he'd made…never mind they didn't know what his true reason was for being in Evergreen…they would find out soon enough…it repulsed him to know that he found himself thinking of Kim and the others as friends, yet they caused the deaths of his two best assassins…once he had the intel, they would all be killed…by him personally…his revenge…and Director James Tilton was now on his target list…simply because he was a great friend and 'family' of the rest of them…their protector of sorts… but could he actually kill anyone…he'd never done so in the past…

Dmitry bid his time with careful planning. Only a few framed paintings were left for him to study in Kim's art gallery, those painted by her mother and not bought at the London art showing. *If only London had worked out…*

He knew the cache of intelligence was nearby, at the gallery. The two he wanted could be in Kim's home, too, since she had some of her mother's paintings hanging there as well. It was harder to look at those in Kim's house that closely, or as carefully since it was dinner and guest time for chatting. Kim had paintings in other rooms that he had not been shown before, too.

Thus, he planned to pop into the gallery more often in the coming weeks, and hopefully ascertain the ideal time to break into her and Paul's home. He might catch words exchanged for when they would attend a concert, do some holiday event, or another home dinner not in Evergreen.

He was patient…he knew what was at stake…he knew how to tell if anything was tucked into the area where the wood joined…or so he thought…he was confident…and a patient man…

Chapter Seventeen

*N*ovember arrived and with it, there was more frustration on the part of Director James Tilson. He did his best to figure out how the art frames were connected to the dead assassin. Still puzzled, he decided to drive up the canyon to Evergreen as he thought a connection may turn up yet, and he missed his family, Kim and Paul, Nancy, Richard, and soon to be born grandson.

When he walked into the art gallery, he caught Kim hanging a new piece on the wall with a very pregnant Nancy holding her in place on a step stool. "I will take over, Nancy. You take a rest in that chair near the window."

She complied with his request as she was less than six weeks away from her delivery date and her back hurt. It was worth it, though, as that tiny human boy would be born soon, and all the aches and pains would be forgotten.

"Thank you, James. What brings you to Evergreen at this time of the morning? It is always great to see you." Kim hugged James briefly before going to their new coffee nook to brew a pot of coffee.

"This coffee nook area is new, isn't it? I did not see it the last time I was here." James smiled at Kim and waited for her to reply.

"Actually, I built it myself, James," Richard responded as he came back into the main gallery space. "I am happy you approve of my design. Great to see you again. People like this nook area and I have been up to my eyeballs in work." Richard chuckled and Nancy snorted.

"Yes, Richard is quite full of himself," she laughed. "But it is true. The coffee nook has brought on more work than he can get to right away, so he has a waiting list. He best not be carving a nook when I go into labor," Nancy eyed Richard with a wink.

"You are talented with wood carving, that's for sure," James smiled, then suddenly he frowned. *Why didn't this idea come to me sooner? Maybe? Might? Does not hurt to ask...*

"What is with the all-of-a-sudden-frown on your face? What is wrong?" Richard asked James as he motioned for him to have a seat at the cozy nook.

Looking sheepish, James replied that he had just had a sudden realization hit him. "I should have asked this months ago and it shames me to no end, especially if I'm right." He took a deep breath.

Kim, Nancy, and Paul wore quizzical expressions as they had no clue what James was referring to.

"Could I see one of the smaller paintings your mom created Kim? At the nook and in the sunlight would be excellent." He suggested.

Kim retrieved a beautiful scenic 9" x 12" landscape of autumn trees with the evening sunlight rays lighting up the leaves and handed it to James.

James carefully looked over the frame and he did not notice anything unusual. "This is a lovely painting. Your mom was talented, Kim, and so are you."

James looked at Richard, and replied, "Richard, an idea popped into my head when I saw the new coffee nook. I do not see anything visually to show if something is inside this frame. What do you use on wood to detect metal or a metallic piece of anything in the wood you carve?

Stunned for just a moment, Richard said he used a special, and extremely sensitive, woodworking metal detector and that it had been in the back room of the gallery since he built the nook last week. "What are you suggesting, James? I am curious."

"You could run that special, extremely sensitive detector over the frame on this piece of beautiful art. No damage would occur in the process. I know it will pick up the V-nails placed to hold the frames at 45-degree angles. I am curious about the rest of the frame." James looked into Richard's eyes and immediately went to the back room to get his detector.

Upon coming back out, Richard explained how his metal detector worked. "Mine is a powerful precision hand-held metal detector with automatic tuning and a laser indicator designed specifically for wood-workers. It helps detect small metal objects hidden inside new or used lumber that I work with."

"Would you scan this frame, please? Nothing will come of it, but if my idea is right, all the frames on your mom's paintings could be checked this way, Kim. We could find out why the frame was taken here at the gallery last July, and why your parents' home was broken into, and certain frames taken, with the paintings left behind, unharmed. Only an art aficionado would do it in this manner, not just any person."

Richard sat down and James handed the small painting over to Richard. Richard turned on his hand detector and started to scan the wooden frame. Kim was quite curious and so was Nancy as they watched Richard scan and what the computer screen on his device showed.

Dmitry walked in the front door with his usual cheery and friendly greeting. Then he saw what Richard was doing and lost his smile, just like that! *No, no you cannot...I am so close...it is my intel...not yours...oh, no...I can distract them...I must...this is not good at all...I must have both pieces of intel...*

"Are you looking for gold or hidden treasure, Richard?" he asked in a joking manner along with a small laugh. *I hope they buy my pitiful joke...any other time I can joke with ease...but this scan of the frame, it is too much...too sudden...no...become organized now...*

Richard stopped scanning, smiled at Dmitry, and replied that he was checking the joints of frames from locals in the gallery. He explained that quality work was important to all of them, and he was only doing the new arrivals as the rest had been done in the past.

Why did I say that? Dmitry tried to joke but I saw him in the corner of my eye... he is not what he projects...he is rich and a Russian oligarch and all of that, but he is a bit more...he is upset with me scanning the frames for sure...but why?

James had caught the look between Richard and Dmitry. Dmitry was nailed, even though he was not. Not yet anyway. And maybe not at all. "Would you like a cup of coffee, Dmitry? Kim just made a fresh pot." Kim grabbed a mug and set it before Dmitry along with some fresh baked shortbread cookies.

Normal conversation returned and Nancy reminded Dmitry that he was invited to celebrate an American Thanksgiving with the Leawood family this year. "You will love tasty food, and great company. It is a special holiday for Americans, and anyone in the USA, if they desire to celebrate. Did you reply to Sarah yet?"

Why did I ask that? Hopefully...Dmitry will see this as a genial conversation, and nothing hidden by anyone...must keep cool...maintain lightness and friendship...

"Why, yes, I did reply in the affirmative, and I look forward to eating and being with all of you." Dmitry gave off a genuine smile, or he faked it in an expert manner. Finally, Dmitry decided on a painting to purchase. It was wrapped, taped up, and he left after saying goodbye.

I hope that's all Richard was doing...making sure the frame joints are quality...it does make sense...and they were so friendly with me...I didn't see any art missing from the walls, but I only had time for a cursory glance...I must play this cool...Moscow is counting on me...Ivan Smirnov is counting on me...

"He's gone, thank goodness." James sounded relieved. "I do not trust him now as I received bad vibes from Dmitry, and I do not know why. He could simply be an egotistic Russian oligarch. Let us finish scanning this frame, Richard. We could be on to something important."

Kim immediately locked the door and flipped the open sign to closed after Dmitry's *Bentley*, with him behind the wheel, drove away. She was nervous and so was Nancy. Both women sat together in the nook and waited for Richard to complete the scan.

Please stay away for now...please be a nice person...please do not be part of the assassins that took out my parents and four friends...please do not be the person who tried to kill my husband in the canyon accident...who wants all of us taken out...

"Bingo!" Richard half yelled. "Right here folks. See for yourself." Plain as day, the scanner screen showed a tiny piece of a partly metallic thing-of-unknown-etiology-or-whatever-it-was inside the frame a few inches from the V-nails on one side piece.

"Please take the frame apart with great care to not damage the painting. Once it is off, do you have a tool with you to chip away the wood from what is inside, Richard?" James was curious. He had to know. He glanced at his three friends, then called for back up from the Denver Federal Center just in case Dmitry came back.

Dmitry could be innocent, though…or not…if not, he could come back with dangerous and deadly intent and force…caution is best… this might be the break we have needed for a long time now…

"Try not to worry. Kim, you look shell shocked, and Nancy, you are not much better. Please sit down and we will know what to do soon." Both ladies sat down, and Richard came back with some of his special woodworking tools.

He slowly chipped away the wood layers until he saw it! "Wow! That looks like an extremely expensive computer chip to me." James caught the look on Richard's face.

"You did this in an extremely professional fashion, Richard. Thank you. Homeland Security and the FBI will be here shortly, and they will take the wood with the chip to the fed center in an armored SUV." James responded.

Both women were glad to see Homeland Security and the FBI pull up and Kim unlocked the door to let them in. Two of them stayed out front guarding the business and those within it.

"How could this tiny chip get inside this frame? And why? This does not make sense. Unless some of the frames were added to mom's paintings on site at the gallery in London? And a spy of some sort framed those pieces? It could have been done at night and a spy could have added the chip in and reframed the art!" Kim looked both Richard and James in the eye.

She dared James to think she was a drama queen…she knew her parents were taken out…as a hit…killed…not an accident…they were taken out…it all made sense…but how much intel and what kind of intel could a chip hold?

"You just made the next connection, Kim. Beautiful, smart, clever, and artistic. I am so enormously proud you are my bonus daughter." James smiled warmly at Kim.

One of the agents brought inside a silver hard sided *Haliburton* briefcase, the kind that is hard to break into, and used two keys and an encryption code. "Sir. What can I do for you?" the agent asked James.

"This piece of wood needs to go inside that case in a careful manner. Do you see the set of microminiaturized electronic circuits on this computer chip in the wood? Chips drive the industry; they are inside most all electronic devices on planet Earth. This one contains top secret information of some sort, and we must be careful to retain the intel, if any, on the chip."

"Yes, Sir. I do see it." The agent opened the metal briefcase and James carefully placed the wood with the chip still in place between two soft, black foam layers to protect it, then he locked the case.

James instructed the agents, "Take this briefcase back to the fed center ASAP and keep it guarded until I can get back and decide the next steps, please." The guards complied with the orders and left.

"Why don't you reopen the gallery, Kim, and do business as usual? Do not scan anymore frames until we know what we are dealing with. If Dmitry comes back, do not be afraid, act like normal, treat him to lunch next door or dinner this evening, act like usual. He will not suspect we are onto anything at all. Put away your tools, Richard. Act normal, you are all old hands at this by now." With that, James departed for the drive back to Lakewood as he followed the armored SUVs.

Dmitry thought over the friendly and cheerful exchange of words at the art gallery. He decided things were okay, for now. But he would watch the gallery a bit closer, visit more often, just to be sure. The intel was too important. *If only London had worked out...but the agents were not able to get the intel retrieved in time...*

Director James Tilson looked at the piece of wood with a chip embedded within it. He had called the head of the FBI in Washington, DC, and that director sent his top people to the fed center in Denver. Once the special team arrived, measures would be taken to safely remove the chip and then try to break its encryption code which could take a day or several months.

Chapter Eighteen

Thirty floors beneath ground level at the Denver Federal Center, Director James Tilson watched as the chip was carefully extracted from the wood. Colonel Jack Ness specialized in extreme top secret intel extraction for the National Security Agency (NSA) and his boss was the General who headed the NSA. The NSA parent agency was the Department of Defense.

Finally, the colonel could work on decryption. Director Tilson left the decryption work to Colonel Jack Ness and went back to his office on the surface. *Who knows how long this will take…or what is on the chip…but it is safely guarded here…safer here than to fly it to DC for decryption…no reason to risk losing the chip…*

Director Tilson was patient in waiting to find out if that chip could be decrypted. Colonel Ness had the job done in just over four hours and then Director Tilson went back down to review the intel with Colonel Jack Ness.

Both men reviewed and discussed the intel in full. The chip held intel on the North American Aerospace Defense Command also known as NORAD. NORAD is a binational treaty-level defense agreement between Canada and the US, to conduct aerospace warning and control for North America.

Most people know that NORAD exists, that it is top-secret, and located inside a mountain, Cheyenne Mountain to be exact, in Colorado Springs, CO. It was built during the height of the Cold War in the late 1950s. The command-and-control center was hard for long-range

Soviet bombers to reach, as it was in the middle of the United States of America.

Since 9/11, (the al-Qaeda the twin towers in New York City, an empty field in Pennsylvania, and the Pentagon) tours were stopped. NORAD is still open for business. *Nothing new here…let us see what else they know…Tilson wanted to know how far they got with the intel…*

At this point in time, NORAD houses many other military operations including the U.S. Strategic Command, U.S. Air Force Space Command and U.S. Northern Command (USNORTHCOM). The main command center moved base to Peterson Air Force Base, fifteen miles away. *So far, no top-secret intel…we are going to be lucky…Tilson was hoping on a wing and a prayer…*

Cheyenne Mountain Complex is still NORAD and USNORTH-COM's Alternate Command Center. NORAD houses more than a dozen different government and Department of Defense agencies inside, and sadly the top-secret ones were listed. *How did they get the list of the top-secret agencies? Absolutely no one in the public sector, and many who were employed at NORAD, were not aware these agencies existed anywhere in the world, not at all…he did not even know until now!*

Director Tilson looked Colonel Ness in the eye. "No one in the public sector knows about these top-secret agencies. How did they obtain that intel?"

"Keep reading, Director, it gets worse." Colonel Ness wanted the director to read the true ramifications of what he had found.

The mountain houses fifteen buildings that are more than a mile inside the mountain and over 2,000 feet down from the top of the mountain. Thirteen 3-floor and two 2-floor free-standing buildings. *Connected by halls and ramps…more than 1300 giant springs…if hit by a blast or an earthquake no damage would occur…the walls would never move enough to touch the tunnel rock…most seismic-sound area of Colorado…nothing top-secret there…*

"This goes into more detail about the mountain, doesn't it Colonel?"

"Yes, Director. Please keep reading so you understand my concern about this. I have not informed my general, yet. I need to discuss it with you first."

The main tunnel is two miles long and has both a north and south portal. The tunnel is curved so it does not go into any veins of gold near Divide, CO. There are two 23-ton blast doors between the main tunnel and the office buildings complex. Both doors remain open but are evaluated each day. Approximately 350 people work inside the complex during the daytime Monday through Friday, and around 125 on nights and weekends. *Nothing top-secret here…hm…*

If necessary, the mountain could accommodate six hundred or more people if war or a bombing was imminent. Workers monitor a lot of scopes and screens, and the mountain houses its own firefighters, indoor and outdoor security, of course, and medical needs. Amenities include a gym, workout facility, spin gym, hospital, chapel, convenience store, and more since those working cannot leave for a meal or walk outside for exercise. *So far, so good…but those top-secret agencies listed above is a true problem…the colonel has not told his general yet…I wonder why…*

The five human-caused lakes, one of which is full of diesel fuel for backup generators, is self-contained. All of it is built using top Navy-grade steel. The high levels of top-secret protection details continued until he read a list of names. They were Russian names, agents of some sort, or assassins, all of them nefarious.

It was difficult to shock Director Tilson, but this list of names, and top-secret protection details were too much…the country was at stake and thus far, no intel was obtained to try and stop whatever nefarious plans had been made or were to be made…that is what got Tilson's gut! Those are top-secret! The extra top-secret tunnels connecting the mountain to more than one airport and military bases…to the Denver Federal Center…to other places…the immense proportion of the network of tunnels…no…who and how did they obtain this intel? Then it dawned on him… someone at the Pentagon was involved…a high ranking official…it had to be… the intel included intel that even he did not know existed…and he had Air Force One clearance! It was now time to make decisions…only one man could decide the right move with those he truly trusted…now we know why there is a hit out on the president…

Director Tilson sat back in his chair and asked the colonel for his opinion both officially and his gut feeling.

"I am afraid my general could be involved. He directed me to report directly to him, and I was instructed to say absolutely nothing to you about any intel I was able to retrieve. That is my official and professional opinion, and my gut tells me the same. My general knows your clearance is as high as Air Force One. Something is not right. It does not sit well in my thoughts, too suspicious." Colonel Ness responded in a sad tone of voice.

"My general must be involved. He will realize at some point that I am on to him. That compromises me and it does not sit well in my stomach. I need advice on what to do ASAP, please.

Tilson studied the colonel's eyes and demeanor before replying, "I trust your reasoning and so we must take this in a different direction. It is time to call the commander-in-chief. I will call from down here right now, and we will have a three-way conversation within this enclosed and well-sealed room, and with this special red phone that goes directly to the commander-in-chief. The conversation must remain utterly top-secret."

The director made the call, and all three men discussed what had been found, and why the general was not informed. Listed in the report were things and items that the president did not know existed, and he stopped them a few times and told them NOT to tell him about 'this or that'.

The president explained that was how it worked, so that the president would have plausible deniability on details he did not need to know, so he could not answer probing questions from the media or anyone at all.

Then he decided on a course of action and informed both men in the manner he wanted the chip to be stored for safety, and security, in a special room and place, at the fed center that Director Tilson did not know existed!

They left the commander-in-chief to deal with the intel as he saw fit, and Colonel Ness was directed to inform his general that the chip had been too damaged to gain intel - per the commander-in-chief!

After securing the chip in the top-secret desired location, Director Tilson went back to his office and Colonel Ness was directed to head back to his office in DC the next day. Both were relieved to leave the situation with the president.

Colonel Ness then informed his general via telephone that the chip had been too damaged to gain intel. The general's voice was icy cold in return. *Does he suspect anything? Did someone tell him of the secret three-way call with the president? He might think I am lying!*

Cybersecurity for both the United States and Canada was at risk and the commander-in-chief had to make fast decisions, while working in tandem with Canada! And Canada had to have a trustworthy and high-ranking individual…time was crucial…in the wrong hands…and two more chips were somewhere…

In DC, the pressure had been too much, and the general took himself out of the equation, by offing himself at home that evening with a handgun. No note was found.

The news made headlines for months to come…what a mess…the lost intel from the general was no longer a thing…his work computer and home computers had been wiped clean or destroyed…and it was evident that the general took himself out OR an assassin took him out and planted the gun in a position of suicide…not that the public was aware of that fact…as it was reported as self-inflicted…

Colonel Ness was promoted to General Ness and became the new head of his department.

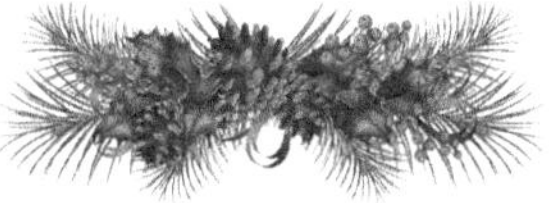

Dmitry wasn't sure what to do…his contact stateside was now dead… intel had not been forthcoming…either no intel was received…or Dmitry was thought to be compromised…the complications maddened him…must stay calm…be the Russian you were born to be…the one heavily trained in special tactics and more…the expert…keep that persona inside and remain the nice, rich, oligarch from Russia…that he could do with aplomb…

Chapter Nineteen

*I*t was Thanksgiving Day and guests were arriving at the Leawood home in Lakewood. The wind was light and large feather-like snowflakes softly fell.

Kim and Paul arrived first, followed by Nancy and Richard. Danny and Lisa bounded out of the house with their parents following. Sarah gave hugs to each, and Aaron motioned everyone inside their home.

As Aaron closed the door, he spotted James pulling up and Dmitry was not far behind. *The gang is here then…hopefully things will go off without a hitch today…*

Aaron and Sarah owned a large and beautiful timbered and river rock home in Lakewood. Soon, everyone was settled around the spacious living room near to a roaring fireplace. A tall and unadorned Christmas tree stood as a lone sentinel in one corner begging to be decorated.

Sadie brought in a trolley loaded with coffee and hot cocoa for the children. Danny was growing fast and would turn age 13 – teenager - on December 12th. Lisa was nine going on twenty-one, or so it seemed.

"Your home always amazes me no matter how often I visit." Kim stated in a cheery manner and voice. "I love the timbers and river rock, and, as you know our condominium is set up similar in that manner. But we do not have all the space that you do. We do not have the small lake, stream, Sadie's cottage, Alice's cottage, and outbuildings like you do."

"I'm with Kim on that one and I love your mini white fairy lights that light up the paths to the cottages and around your home." Nancy lowered herself into a soft and cozy recliner and up went her feet. Her baby bump was prominent, and she looked radiant.

Sadie had gone back into the kitchen with Alice not far behind her. The feast needed to be checked and the kitchen was the heart of the Leawood home. Soon, James would come looking for Alice, he always did.

Those two are a match made in heaven…both Aaron and Sarah had discussed this aspect recently and they were delighted. Aaron's mother, Alice, might just gain a new husband…she had been without one for an extraordinarily long time…since she was widowed at a young age…left to raise two children…

The kitchen was cheery and evoked a sense of home, safety, and security. Oak cabinets and granite counter tops matched the island in the middle. Black and chrome appliances fit in perfectly.

Through the floor to ceiling picture windows, two small cottages, some outbuildings, and a small, but entirely lovely, lake fed by a small stream, gave everyone a magnificent view with the gently falling snow.

Sarah had given everyone a tour of their home in the past, but Dmitry had not received a tour yet. "Care to tour the rest of our home, Dmitry? We have time before the meal is ready."

Dmitry smiled, "Sure. That sounds great!"

"I'll come along, too." Aaron said, "I don't want Dmitry to try and steal you away from me." Everyone had a great laugh over that one.

Sarah had decided on a shortened and abbreviated tour. "Let us begin the tour! This is where all things winter goes," Sarah smiled as they walked into the mud room. "In here is where all our outdoor gear such as snowshoes, ski equipment, ice skates, and heavy outerwear are kept. We have a lot of equipment for winter sports."

Sarah led Dmitry and Aaron to the laundry room as she explained that all summer sports gear had its own shed behind the main house. A door led outside to a deck area that was handy for placing extra muddy and grimy gear, before stepping inside the mud room.

Back up the hall and through the open kitchen to the dining room, she went as the men followed. Exposed beams in the vaulted ceiling gave warmth to the room, which was dominated by a large gleaming rectangular pecan dining table that sat twelve people with ease. Matching chairs surrounded the table that was decorated with candles and autumn decorations, gourds, small pumpkins, and fake pine branches.

The soft lighting above the table leant an air of coziness to the overall room. Family pictures graced the walls, and a set of bay windows surrounded a breakfast/reading nook, which easily seated five or six people. Soft rose-colored cushions created a perfect place to read, snack, drink coffee, or daydream. Oak herringbone wood flooring completed the spacious room.

"This is rather lovely, a sense of home, the photographs complement the room nicely," Dmitry said with a genuine smile.

Or it was genuine…with him one never truly knew…

"Thank you! We aim to have our home family oriented, as family is precious to us both, to all of us here right now." Sarah gave Dmitry a smile. "Shall we continue?"

Sarah went through a curved arch and into the main living room they had been in earlier when they arrived.

The first door on the right was the master bedroom with an ensuite and a lovely fireplace. A king sized, carved, dark mahogany, four-poster bed dominated the room, with matching carved tables on either side of the bed that was covered in a plush autumn duvet, and decorative pillows.

Two walk-in closets completed the master suite and the oak walls held photos of happy family times along with pictures of a five-year-old blonde headed little boy along with the same little boy without hair.

Not going there with Dmitry…nope…not going to happen…never…ever…no spoiling of my little boy with Dmitry…Simon had only been age five-years-old when he died a terrible and utterly painful death!

"Further down the hall and on the right is Aaron's den," Sarah pointed out. "Please don't enter this room as Aaron makes notes regarding patients now and then, and patient privacy is highly important."

Across the hall was a full bath next to the playroom. Sarah smiled as she showed the way to the open room filled with books, toys, and a computer for Danny and Lisa.

"Aaron and I prefer to have the children near us when they are playing. We can hear them laugh and giggle, yet still watch a movie or listen to music as we discuss our day at work or events around the world. This room is called *Danny and Lisa,* and the kids love having the room named after them." Sarah smiled as Dmitry stepped away from the room.

"Lately, Danny has been with his boy scout friends more and more, and he is working on his Eagle Scout rank. We are so proud of what he has attained in his young life, and he soars being out in nature and around other people." Sarah thought unto herself as she remembered many past events that had shaped the life of her son.

The abuse his father doled out every single day…Danny had been part of her messy divorce with his father…and losing his younger brother to cancer at only age five years…past events had changed them…now Danny was able to talk about what he saw, thought, or heard…Aaron had reached him…and Danny finally felt secure…

Back in the entryway, Sarah pointed out a large, carved, and curved, mahogany staircase with the balustrade decorated in fake pine boughs, autumn décor, and fairy lights. The stairway was covered in light brown carpeting.

"We do not have time to tour the upstairs, but we have six bedrooms, some with ensuites, and two with a connecting bathroom for the children. We have an attic reached by a staircase at the end of the second-floor hallway and a lot of seasonal decorations and the like are stored up there."

Sarah walked over to another door on the first floor and pointed at it. "This door leads to our basement. We use it for storage, too, and we have a second laundry room as well. Next to it is another door that goes into our pantry. And that is the tour, Dmitry." Sarah gave Dmitry a huge smile as she accepted a kiss on the top of her head from her husband.

"Thank you for giving me a tour. Your home is lovely, and you are talented in your taste of furnishings." Dmitry smiled at both Aaron and Sarah as they walked back into the main living room space.

Lovely couple…lovely home…a boy not here…had been sick…no hair…cancer in a child is sad…but I can't let that affect me…I just can't allow myself to honestly like these people…I have my orders and those orders include 'whatever means necessary'…collateral damage…hmmm…stop it now, Dmitry! Do not go all soft… remember who and what you are…

The smells that emanated from the kitchen made Aaron's tummy growl and Lisa laughed when Sarah snickered aloud.

"Dinners ready," announced Sadie. The roasted turkey came out perfect – it always did when Sadie cooked it. She also made homemade dinner rolls to go along with the turkey and gravy. This year, eleven people graced the dining room table. Aaron would carve the bird like usual once the food was on the table and the sideboard. It was a moment of pride and tradition for him to carve the bird after prayers were said.

Both Alice and Sarah had helped with the meal prep. Alice created homemade cranberry sauce, sage dressing, and green bean casserole. Sarah roasted sweet potatoes, ultra-fluffy mashed potatoes, and a green bean casserole dish.

Kim had dropped off the desert dishes yesterday, that Nancy and she had made for the meal. The women had baked pumpkin, cherry, and pecan pies, and a sinfully divine pumpkin cheesecake. They were on the sideboard and waited to be eaten after the meal.

Coffee, tea, hot cocoa, and fruit juice rounded out the meal.

"It is time to eat everyone. Sit wherever you wish at the table. Aaron, you have the head spot with the turkey like always." Sarah rang a tiny bell and announced the meal was ready.

Once seated, Aaron gave the blessing and thankfulness for their meal and the richness of family and friends gathered at the table. The blessing included thanks for what each of them had overcome this year and blessings yet to come.

Aaron carved the turkey while the others passed around side dishes. The ambiance of being one big and happy family was in the air.

The desserts were a huge hit all around. The women along with Aaron and Paul helped with cleanup and the kids helped load the dishwasher with the first load of the day.

Back in the main living area, they gathered near the roaring fire, contentment on their faces. Darkness was setting in fast on this side of the continental divide, and with it, the snow had stopped, and Dmitry caught sight of two deer in the snow from the main windows.

"The deer makes it hard to go back home but I must. Once they are in the woods, anyway." Dmitry commented. He was the first to say goodbye as he left for home, this time driving a new black SUV and not his *Bentley*.

Richard was eager to get Nancy home, as she was overtired from the day, and dark circles shone clearly under her blue eyes. He wanted Nancy and their little nugget back home and cozy so off they went.

Kim and Paul were the next ones to say goodbye. They were anxious to get back home, and 'practice' creating a baby of their own. Paul wanted to 'practice' as often as possible, and both simply loved having each other to love. They were blessed. If a baby were conceived then great, if not, they would do what was needed to have a child of their own. It mattered not if Kim carried a baby to delivery, they could adopt. They decided to give it more time.

Kim's back was doing well with the nerve stimulation device that was implanted in her back about a year ago. Her lower back pain peaked at a 6 on a 1 − 10 scale and was usually around 4 most of the time. What a change from one year ago and topping out above 10 much of the time.

Sadie said goodbye after starting the second load of dishes in the dishwasher. She was ready to head for her cottage behind the main house. Alice also said goodbye as she did not want Sadie to walk to her cottage alone and Richard was eager to escort both women to their cottages.

Both Danny and Lisa took themselves off to bed, it had been a full day, and they were tired.

"Just you and me, Babe. Just us and the cozy fire with a few candles lit." Aaron kissed Sarah's sweet lips and the kiss deepened along with roving hands here and there.

"A perfect ending to a most wonderful day," Sarah looked at Aaron before she blew out the candles, then she said, "Race you to the shower!" and they both went up to their bedroom ensuite for some soapy and sensual sex, loving each other in the way only those truly in love can do.

Chapter Twenty

Richard had finished the beautiful carved wood Victorian-style bassinet and crib by the first of December. He had used seasoned pine wood for both pieces as pine wood provides safety and stability, thus meeting the necessary standards for supporting a baby's weight.

Richard knew the pine wood would be durable and less prone to cracking or splintering. The carved wood was elegant with graceful curves, yet simple in design.

When he created the crib, Richard made sure that it would convert to a toddler bed, at the right time. The sealant on the wood was officially baby approved, and no paint was used.

The wood would show dings and scratches since it was pine, but that shows a well-used baby crib for a well-loved baby. Nancy had both the bassinet and crib set up with soft sheets and baby safe bedding. For now, a soft blue teddy bear lay in place of their baby-to-be-born.

December 12 arrived and with it, Danny turned 13 – a teenager! He chose to invite six scouting friends over for his special day. They would have dinner and cake, followed by birthday gifts and then all-things-pinewood-derby.

Aaron answered the doorbell when it rang and found Dmitry outside – an unexpected visit. "Hello Dmitry. Care to come inside?"

"Yes, please, Aaron. I have a gift for Danny. I know he turned 13 today and I wanted to surprise him." Dmitry gave off a genuine smile and that was his façade, his modus operandi.

"Come on in. Danny has friends over for his birthday, and then they have Pinewood Derby cars to create." Aaron welcomed Dmitry into his home and called for Danny.

"What is up, Dad? Oh. Hi Mr. Ivanov." Danny smiled.

"I have brought you a surprise gift for your birthday. Please open it up." Dmitry gazed at Danny expectantly.

"Thank you. This is a surprise. You did not have to buy me any-thing." Danny started to peel the wrapping off the box.

"I know I didn't have to, but I wanted to." Dmitry smiled and stud-ied Danny as he opened his gift.

"Wow!" Danny replied as he found a cool tech item – a Mini Drone with Camera, 720P HD FPV Foldable Drones, 2 Batteries, One Key Start, Headless Mode, Altitude Hold, and with a 360 Flip. A great beginner's drone, for games and camera shots. Total battery time was 22 minutes, and the range was up to 130 feet.

Thank you, Mr. Ivanov." Danny grinned at Dmitry.

"Welcome, Danny. I am sure you will have hours of fun with it. I know you have a party to attend with your friends, so I will be off now. Goodbye."

"Goodbye, Dmitry," Aaron responded before closing the front door.

Ah…plan worked like a charm…Danny would use that drone and never know that he was being spied on when in use, and not in use…a nice tiny spy device that no one would notice…Dmitry thought he had the perfect way to monitor conversations of any importance to his mission…Danny and his family would never know they were being spied on…one step closer in gaining the intel he desperately needed…he thought about other places he could place a spy device chip in secret…the art gallery was next on his list…

It was on! Each young teenager was eager to start to work on their Pinewood Derby cars! Danny looked forward to the derby each year and he felt special knowing that the derby is for Cub and Boy Scouts only. The scouts build a derby car, and they race the cars down a sloped track, two cars at a time until the winners are chosen. The faster cars raced more times in a double elimination race.

Aaron wondered if seven boys was too many when they all started talking at once! "Whoa! Slow down you folks! That sugar from the cake has you stirred up. Grab your derby car box and head to the dining room. Once newsprint is laid out over plastic you can start. Deal?" He lifted his right eyebrow.

"Deal!" They replied at the same time, then laughed and Aaron laughed along with them.

Taking places at the table they opened their box. Each box contained one wooden block with plastic wheels and metal axles. They talked about the style and shape of how they wanted their derby car to look like while Aaron went to get his toolbox.

The boys laid out the pieces on the table and Aaron gave them each a sheet of white paper to draw a design of how they wanted their derby car shape to be. This was Aaron's fourth year helping with the Pinewood Derby.

First, they laid the block of soft wood on the paper then drew around it in pencil. Then the real design began as each boy drew with a pencil inside the box for the shape they wanted. Aften much discussion and erasing, they completed the job at hand.

"Look at all of you! You are all old pros at this now. Cut out your car shape and then lay that shape on your wood. Carefully trace around the paper shape." Aaron directed the boys, um…young teenagers.

Once done, Aaron inspected each block of wood. He was satisfied with how they had progressed in their cars this year. One by one, Aaron cut each car out with a small band saw in the garage. "Next year, you might be ready to cut your own cars out."

The boys sipped on hot chocolate while waiting their turn for their car to be cut out and they wore eye protection as directed by Aaron. They inspected each other's car and talked nonstop.

Back in the dining room, it was time for sanding the soft pine wood. The boys were careful and already pros at this part of the process.

"High fives to each of you!" Aaron held out his right hand for the classic high five.

"Have you thought about what color you want your car to be this year? I have a box with small glass paint bottles to choose from. Plent of colors and brushes." Aaron smiled down at the boys as he sipped on hot coffee. He knew the color decision was not going to be fast.

In the interim, he brought out a small kitchen scale to weigh the cars and their parts. "You already know how the tires and axles slide in on the car so now it is time to weigh them with their parts. One boy at a time. Remember, they cannot be over five ounces."

Most of the cars and parts weighed between 2.5 and 3 ounces. Aaron had a selection of small metal weights to add to the cars. It was trial and error before the right metal weight, combined with the cut-out car shape of wood, plastic wheels, and metal axles that looked like four nails, weighed between 4.8 and 4.9 ounces.

Aaron carved an area in the soft wood, on the underside of each car, for the metal weights, and the boys glued theirs in place with a special glue that dried fast.

Sarah peeked into the dining room and saw eight happy faces. *Life was wonderful…with a smile on her face, she went back to the main living room and sat down near the fireplace to read…Lisa was already tucked in bed for the night…*

Once the fast-acting glue was dry, the boys started painting their derby cars with… you guessed it, fast-drying paint. They were careful and painted the bottom of the car first and allowed it to dry for the specified time.

Then the fun began once more. Each boy placed the bottom side of their cars on a glass pedestal, so that they could paint the sides and top of the car. Once done, the cars were left to dry completely, which only meant about a half hour with the special paint.

Finally, the boys took each black plastic wheel and put an axle type of nail in the hole in the middle of each wheel and then slipped each nail into the pre-made slots on their cars. The wheels moved freely as they assessed each car carefully.

Ta Da! Done. The cars were safely stored in shoe boxes to take back home in the morning. All seven boys spent the night in the play-room in nice warm sleeping bags and soft pillows. They were sound asleep by midnight.

Aaron found Sarah in their bedroom. Sarah wore a see-through, barely there, red baby doll nightie that spoke to him. Quick as a flash he took a shower and slipped into bed with his wife. Aaron kissed every single inch of her, breathed softly in her ears and that always drove Sarah wild! His vixen came to life and her wildness consumed him completely; he finally entered her, and they made beautiful love together, in perfect rhythm, leaving his seed inside her, making a baby. Another perfect ending to a perfect day. Sated and content, they fell asleep in each other's arms.

Chapter Twenty-One

*D*irector Tilson worked closely with General Ness as their investigation was ongoing and they were looking at anything remotely connected with the dead Russian spy and the general who had offed himself. Both knew the two men were connected.

The cybersecurity consequences for both the United States and Canada were yet to be known…no matter how much preparation was planned…and one more chip was somewhere…the news still speculated about the death of Ness' ex-general in DC…why he'd taken his own life…the news outlets spoke of depression often…it was easier to let them think it was depression…the reality was too much…and the public could never know most details…

The break came on Saturday, 19 December! Scotland Yard had caught Olga Pasternak, who had worked with frames and framing at all the London gallery shows, on a secret spy camera device they had set up with the United States, General Ness, and the Brigadier General at Ramstein Air Base in Germany.

Olga Pasternak was caught reframing a painting for the current London showing. The painting did not need reframing. She had chosen a small landscape painting like the one Kim's mother had painted, the one that they had found the first high tech chip inside of, with the intel on the Federal Center, NORAD, and tunnels under metro Denver people did not know existed!

Using Richard Manse's method of scanning frames, an agent quickly scanned the frame Olga Pasternack had reframed, when she was engaged in gallery talk in the main gallery, and the agent found a chip!

Olga Pasternak was arrested and detained. The framed piece was placed inside a hard silver locked metal case cushioned with black foam and secured at Ramstein Air Base in the state of Rheinland-Pfalz in the southwest corner of Germany, and with the Brigadier General.

On General Ness's orders, via the commander-in-chief, a C-37A/B twin-engine, turbofan aircraft was ordered to prepare for receiving and delivering the hard silver locked metal case, the Brigadier General's second in command, four special ops (operations) ranking members of the aircraft division, four high ranking guards, and a hand-cuffed Olga Pasternak, all to be flown directly to Denver and would be met on the tarmac upon arrival.

No one on the flight knew the mission details as it was exceptionally top-secret. Those inside the aircraft did not know what their mission involved, they only knew the plane was headed to Denver, and that Olga Pasternak, with her shiny handcuffs, and the hard silver locked metal case would be met on the tarmac and delivered to those who awaited them.

General Ness, Director Tilson, and four special ops guards met the plane. The transfer from the plane to the armored military SUVs was without incident and driven directly back to the fed center.

Olga Pasternack was one tough cookie! She was hard to break, and they kept here there, locked up, and guarded, and would for as long as it took to break her and find out what the Russians had in mind. Had she been locked up and detained in DC, word could leak out. DC was also easily reachable, and Denver was not.

Dmitry wasn't sure what to do…his contact stateside was dead…no intel… even worse was the fact that the Russian agent who'd infiltrated Scotland Yard had news…Olga Pasternak had been caught placing a chipped frame onto a painting in London at the art gallery…that intel was unsettling to put it mildly…he needed that chip! He needed Olga Pasternak doing her part…now he was fully alone… Olga Pasternack was kept locked up somewhere…and she could break…the complications maddened him…he must stay calm…be the Russian you were born to be…the one heavily trained in special tactics and more…the expert…keep that persona inside and remain the nice, rich, oligarch from Russia…that he could do with aplomb…until the oligarch above him stopped funding him…and that would mean only one thing…he would then be on that Russians' hit list…best not think about that overly much…

After thinking about Olga Pasternack and intel she could potentially give up for a lighter sentence, plus the fact that at least one computer chip with intel, and possibly both chips were with the United States government, he knew what he had to do, and he had to do it fast.

He had become a liability and he had to protect himself. He would not take his own life like the general. Yes, he was heavily trained in special tactics, and yes, his own oligarch money sat nicely in a Swiss bank account under a holding company that was untouchable. Russia could do absolutely nothing about his Swiss bank account.

Yet he WAS touchable!!! Even though he, himself had never once killed anyone, he had been complicit by his position between those who ordered hits and those who carried them out.

Thus, he packed a bag and drove in his SUV down to Denver, to the Federal Center, and asked at the gate for Director James Tilson, that he, Dmitry Ivanov, had top-secret information for him. One of the guards radioed inside and spoke with the director.

Director Tilson informed the guards that two members of his team would go to the gate and escort Dmitry Ivanov inside.

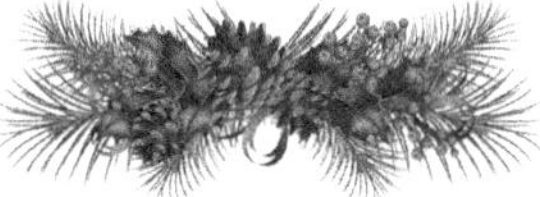

Saturday, December 19, was still crazy with a ton of things going on, and that included the Pinewood Derby. Danny and the whole family were excited as they headed to the scout building to join the others. Aunt Kim, Uncle Paul, Nancy, and Richard, and Grandpa James had been invited, but had to decline citing he had work to do.

Most of the scouts had an abundance of family with them in support. After the official opening of the meeting ended, the announcement of the derby racers was called in pairs to bring their cars to the wooden track.

The scoutmaster had a main list of names paired and the assistant scoutmaster, Aaron helped with the double elimination charting.

It was on! Excitement filled the air. The boys were ready to fly off their seats and race their cars. Danny and his car were doing well thus far.

By the end of the Pinewood Derby, Danny took First Place in Best of Show and Second Place in the derby race itself. Two new trophies. He was all smiles.

The scouts and entourage were enjoying the table refreshments when something ginormous for Danny happened!

Richard noticed Nancy was holding her back and wore a grimace on her face. "What is up, Babe? Is that little gold nugget kicking you again?" He was concerned about both his wife and soon-to-be-born son who was due in six days.

"My back has hurt off and on today. Now, I have sharp pains in my back that are becoming worse and close together. I am in labor!" Nancy looked at Richard's face with alarm. "It's time to head to the hospital."

Richard helped Nancy to stand up and then her waters broke! Right there in the scout cabin in front of all those people! The commotion got the attention of everyone present. Danny was on top of things and rushed to Nancy's side! He was in scout mode all the way and assisted Nancy in getting into the passenger side of her Jeep. *Danny was going to have a brand-new cousin…his first ever cousin…his smiles were of the GINORMOUS size!!!*

Aaron and Sarah were proud of how he helped Nancy, and they knew Danny was in his element.

Kim and Paul also rushed to help Richard with Nancy. Sarah gave Nancy a thumbs up and a huge smile before telling them she would clean up the 'water' on the floor. *How embarrassing that was! But the baby was coming! Now! Six days early!*

Chapter Twenty-Two

Daniel Richard Manse came into the world at 2:20 am on 20 December. All 8 pounds 4 ounces and 20 inches long with dark hair and dark blue eyes, ten fingers and ten toes. He was named after Danny, and Richard both.

Two days later, the new family was ensconced in their mountain home with the fireplace blazing. Nancy sat comfortably on their large dark brown leather wrap-around sofa with comfortable sofa pillows gently rocking the cradle next to her that held their new baby boy. Plenty of windows allowed natural light to filter inside and houseplants thrived.

Nancy and Richard were overjoyed with their new little bundle of love - their special new Christmas gift from the Lord above. Nancy chose to breast feed her new baby and Richard helped all he could.

They were homebodies for now and planned to stay that way until the New Year. They would do Christmas Eve mass from home this year, as illness was in full force and neither wanted their son to get sick.

Nancy did not plan to go back to work at the gallery until February and she would be able to have her son with her during working hours. *Talk about an impressive job! Kim was the absolute best…Kim knew she would get in a lot of baby cuddles…and Nancy was more than happy to oblige her…they had been through so much, thick, and thin, terrifying, and hilarious…*

Emerald eyed Susan Davis worked out nicely at the gallery and she was energetic. Her dark red hair was not easily tamed, and Kim loved how she fit right in, ginger and all. They had grown close and now considered themselves sisters. The family was expanding, and everyone was happy.

On Christmas Eve, the Leawood family along with Alice and Sadie attended church at Light of the World Catholic Church. Director James Tilson sat with the Leawood family, and no one knew about Olga Pasternack or Dmitry Ivanov. *Top secret was top secret!!! Even Olga Pasternak and Dmitry Ivanov did not know where each other was detained… and only one of them was working with and helping General Ness and Director Tilson.*

Finally, Kim and Aaron slipped into the two seats saved for them next to Uncle James. The mass was beautiful, and the Lord's birth celebrated. Christmas Eve Mass was a favorite one for all and so was Easter! Our Savior's birth and His resurrection into Heaven three days after dying on the cross – for our sins!

Afterwards, Paul and Kim left for home and arrived safely at their condominium in Evergreen. They shared an intimate evening in front of the fireplace, thankful for their numerous blessings.

"Care for a glass of wine, Kim?" Paul asked in a husky voice as he nuzzled her neck.

"About that wine, we need to talk." Kim smiled brightly at her husband, radiating joy in her eyes.

"What's up, Babe?" Paul asked his wife as went back to nuzzle a bit more. He did not see the radiance on her face and in her eyes.

"Look at me and I'll tell you," Kim responded, and Paul looked into the eyes of his beautiful wife.

"I am pregnant! You are going to be a daddy!" Kim smiled up at her husband's startled face.

"Wait! What was that? When... How..." Paul stood up, then flopped back down on the sofa abruptly.

"Well, the how you should know since you are a doctor after all and..." Kim broke out in full laughter and Paul laughed with her.

Paul interrupted the laughter with another question, "How far along or do you even know?" He was completely elated to find out that they would be having a baby, and he grinned from ear to ear.

"I took a home pregnancy test and it was positive. I have an appointment with Dr Tammy Harwell, the doctor who delivered Nancy's baby, next week. From my best guess, and using an online due date calculator, I am due around September 6, so I am only a about three weeks or so..." Kim took a deep breath and then relaxed.

Paul pulled Kim onto his lap and cuddled his wife, murmuring sweet nothings into her ear, and then finally taking her to bed for the night – the night he had received the absolute best Christmas present. They spoke of dreams for the future and then fell asleep entwined in each other's arms, happy about the upcoming baby – the perfect Christmas gift they were blessed to receive – the gift that keeps on giving.

The Leawood family and Sadie arrived home, and they sat near the fireplace enjoying the taste of hot cocoa and reflecting on the beautiful Christmas Eve Mass they had just attended.

This year, it would be the Leawood family, Alice, Uncle James, and Sadie spending Christmas Day together. Richard and Nancy were with their little bundle of joy and Kim and Paul had other plans.

The hour was late and the Leawood family shut down their home in favor of bedtime and sleep. Tomorrow will be a busy Christmas Day.

Upon arrival, Uncle James escorted both Sadie and Alice to their respective cottages behind the Leawood home - Christmas Eve was over as it was 11 pm.

James stoked the fireplace while Alice hung up their outwear, in Alice's cottage. The warmth of the fire was welcome, and Alice made hot chamomile tea for both, and she placed the tray on a table next to her soft and cozy sofa before she sat down.

"This is chamomile tea, right? For real? I am game to give it a try," James smiled at Alice, relaxed, and sat down next to her on the sofa. "If it relaxes me, I'll have to go out and buy some." He smiled at Alice.

Alice sipped on her cup and soon they reminisced about the events since last Memorial Day Weekend. A lot had happened that weekend, and since then, too. With time, they had grown closer, and even shared their first kiss a few weeks ago on Thanksgiving – in the Leawood dining room no less, and they had been caught by the children!

That started a round of laughter and giggling for some minutes as they looked at each other and remembered…life was great for both; they were ready to take the next step…

"I have given it consideration, James. I love how our relationship evolved and I am comfortable with it. What do you think of taking it to the next level? I mean, love is not only for young couples. And…" Alice laughed when she saw James grin at her.

"I am thrilled to hear you say that, Alice. I have been wanting the same thing." With that James gave Alice a sweet kiss followed by a searing kiss she would never forget!

People in their fifties could have this kind of relationship, if not, a better one since they did not have children to rear, and the various responsibilities associated with family life.

James yawned, then told Alice that the chamomile tea worked wonders. He was sleepy, indeed.

"You are not driving back home this late. I will show you the guest bedroom and you can sleep there tonight. First, I will put our teacups and tray in the kitchen." Alice refused argument about where James was going to sleep.

"Follow me, please." James did as she asked. Your room is two doors down on the left, and the bathroom is directly across from it. The first door on the right is my room with ensuite.

With that, Alice gave James a goodnight kiss, motioned him toward the guest room, stepped inside her door, and closed said door leaving James in the hallway. *James was a big boy, and he could see himself off to bed…let Aaron and Sarah wonder why they see James' vehicle still parked in their driveway come morning! You are not the only one in love, my dear son. Smiling with contentment, she fell asleep.*

Epilogue

On New Year's Eve, Nancy and Richard's home was invaded by the Leawood family, Sadie, Alice and Uncle James, and Kim with her husband, Paul.

Aaron and Kim Leawood worked hard as a doctor and registered nurse, but they spent a lot of time making memories with Danny and Lisa. Sadie often joined in with the adventures.

Danny and Lisa Leawood were especially happy to meet their new baby cousin, Daniel Richard Manse, only 11 days old! Danny decided he would call his new cousin, Dan.

Kim and Paul announced the news of Kim expecting their first child. She glowed with happiness and a bit of a pregnancy glow. A new baby in 2024 was music to their ears.

Uncle James became known as Grandpa James due to 11 days old Daniel Richard Manse. James and Aaron's mother, Alice, officially let the world know that they were a couple! Who said people in their fifties could not fall in love?

Olga Pasternak ended up being deported back to Russia and left in Russia's hands as to her fate. No intel was gleaned before she was deported.

Dmitry Ivanov's existence will be a major plot in book three of this trilogy, Heart of Evergreen.

Note: Russian spies are located all over the United States. These spies blended seamlessly as part of the USA culture. They live and work among us, as neighbors and co-workers. They fit the ideal of an American family. Many often lived in pairs so they could, "live amongst the enemy and blend in and not stand out" and they often used Morse code in reporting back to Russia. Current estimates place the number of Russian spies operating in the USA between 2,000 and 3,000, which could be much higher. This is the society in which we live.

City of Spies: DC Is the World Capital of Espionage. The Denver Federal Center was harder, by far, to infiltrate.

Biography

*M*ary L. Schmidt writes under the name of S. Jackson along with her husband, pen name A Raymond, and Mary L. Schmidt. She grew up in a small Kansas (USA) town and has lived in more than one state since then. At this time, Ms. Schmidt and her husband split their time between Kansas and Colorado (they love the mountains and off-road 4-wheeling). Traveling is one of their most favorite things to do and she always has a book or even three books to read, in the same week. Books have always been her thing. It seemed like every time she turned around, a new library card was needed due to the current one being stamped completed. Diving into a good book made any day perfect and you would be surprised at the number of books she has read over and over. She drew paper dolls and clothes for them, and with watercolor as her medium when painting scenes, especially flowers. She continued with art in high school exploring a wide variety of arts and loved it! Her creative side loves to be an amateur "shutterbug" and they have an online art gallery. In college, she went into the sciences of all things and received a bachelor's degree in the Science of Nursing. Her nursing career was extraordinarily successful, and she hung up her nursing hat in December 2012.

She is a retired registered nurse; a member of the Catholic Church and has taught kindergarten Catechism; she has worked in various capacities for The American Cancer Society, March of Dimes, Cub, and Boy Scouts, (son, Gene, is an Eagle Scout), and sponsored trips for high school music children. She loves all forms of art but mostly focuses on the visual arts, such as amateur photography, traditional, and graphic art as her health allows.

She has written fifty books, this book is number 50, in various genres and has other works in process, along with inclusion in four anthologies.

A. Raymond is a member of the Catholic Church and has helped his wife with The American Cancer Society, March of Dimes, Cub and Boy Scouts, and sponsored children alongside his wife on music trips. He devotes his spare time to fishing, reading, playing poker, Jeeping, and traveling adventures with his wife. Spending time with their grandson, Austin, and granddaughter, Emma, happens to be another favorite past time.

Heart of Evergreen Trilogy

"Upon finding one's name at the top of their husbands's hit list, one must strategize for their survival."

"The assassin left a note at the scene of the two killed. It read, 'Two down, eleven to go' and you are a target!"

Verbiage to come...
Out late 2024!

Memoirs

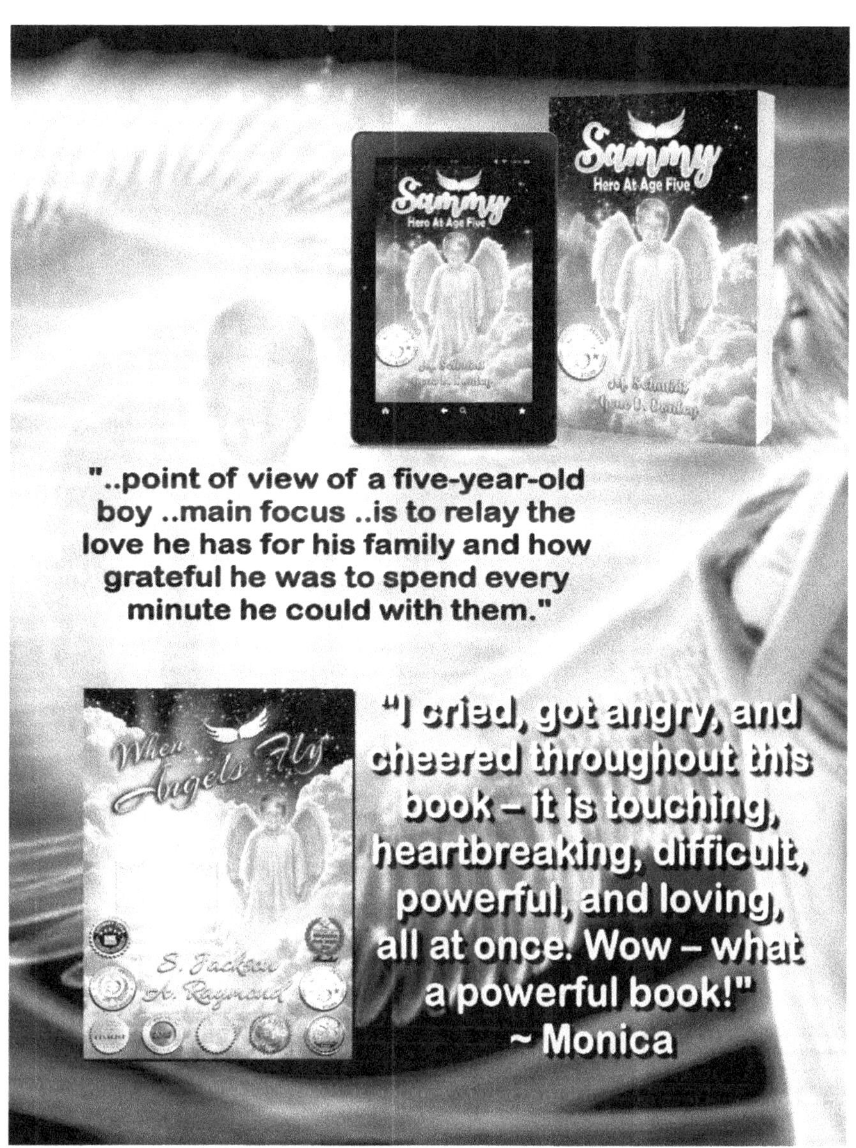

Sammy
Hero At Age Five
Sammy
Hero At Age Five
"..point of view of a five-year-old boy ..main focus ..is to relay the love he has for his family and how grateful he was to spend every minute he could with them."
When Angels Fly
S. Jackson
A. Raynald
"I cried, got angry, and cheered throughout this book – it is touching, heartbreaking, difficult, powerful, and loving, all at once. Wow – what a powerful book!"
~ Monica

Visions of her Cherokee grandmother, Cordie, flashed through Mary's mind as her mother, Marguerite, informed her that her stepfathershot himself and was in the hospital. Oh no!

No! This can't be! Not after the joking around at my home last night. NO!!!!Did she use me last night? She'd never use her scapegoat child. No, she couldn't! Even Marguerite wouldn't sink that low! Or would she? Marguerite had always been abusive and vile to most people,and especially to her children and husbands, but would she shoot Harold?

Yet, here I was, and I had to tell the police that, yes, my mother was at my home all evening and into the night. How despicable that my mother connived her way into using me as her alibi. Her insanity unchecked and never stopped.

This book is a true memoir drawing upon the locals and inspiration of the areas in which the author lives and works. Names of towns, places, facilities, and people are real except for three men. Any resemblance to persons living or dead is not coincidental in nature and places where events take place are from her life growing up and as an adult.

Visions of her Cherokee grandmother, Cordie flashed through Sarah's mind as her abusive husband brutally raped her repeatedly shortly after giving birth. He took what he wanted, leaving her bloody body to be filled with years of physical pain and emotional scars that led her to believe she was worthless, and a happy life was hopeless. Sarah tried many times to leave but that was always futile. She felt useless. Her life was shattered once again when her oldest son, John, died at birth and Simon, her youngest endured a horrific cancer battle. With her only living son, Daniel she felt renewed strength knowing Cordie was watching over them always. She finally had the courage with the help of Cordie's visions from the spirit world to leave her abusive husband and make a new life for her and her son. Her new oath to her and Daniel was that no one would ever hurt either of them. Romantic love never existed for Sarah, although she had room in her heart for love. Life taught her to be wary, until the day an old friend from her past, Aaron came back into her life. Would she finally find and know true love? Could Aaron break through the walls that surrounded her? Dare she hope for love once?

Children's Books

In Davy's Dragon Castle, children learn to get along with others no matter the color of their fur or skin. It's important for children to learn the concept of, and how to not be racist and toddlers are a great age to start the teaching. Anti-racism education in elementary school starts with students' awareness of themselves, of others and of how those interactions play out. All social and emotional learning helps children to express feelings and be tuned in to the needs of others. This teaching contributes to the development of all children. Additionally, children are introduced to a character that wears a prosthetic leg, giving children a chance to learn and understand how prosthetics work and if it does/does not limit abilities. Acceptance and inclusion are important in social learning from an early age.

Tommy Turtle is a shy land turtle who likes to hide inside his shell. Tommy represents children who are shy around other children and adults, and he is nervous to play or speak. Most children are shy from time to time and it's important for children to understand shyness and how to act around others who are or aren't shy. Children need to know that shyness is normal, and they need positive encouragement from peers, family, and teachers/adults in their lives. This concept teaching can start in preschool. Children need to develop and practice social skills which will increase their quality of life in school through drama class, music, gym class, show and tell time, play time and more, rather than staying on the sidelines and simply watching others and having less friends and social isolation. If confidence is learned, self-esteem increases, and children succeed. Less confidence promotes increased shyness. It is essential to praise children for their successes and not shame them at all when they fail. All social and emotional learning helps children to express feelings and be tuned in to the needs of others.

Suzy
Has A
Secret
by
S. Jackson,
A. Raymond & M. Schmidt

The Big
Cheese Festival
by S. Jackson,
A. Raymond, & M. Schmidt

Book 10
Shadow and Friends
Meet
Mr. Rabbit
S. Jackson,
A. Raymond, & M. Schmidt

Book 11
Shadow and Friends
Costume
Party
by
S. Jackson,
A. Raymond & M. Schmidt

Shadow and Friends
Family
Reunion
by
S. Jackson,
A. Raymond & M. Schmidt

Available at Amazon, Walmart, and All Bookstores!